URS

THE NEW WINDMILL SERIES

General Editors: Anne and Ian Serraillier

223

Last Stand at Goodbye Gulch

A Western with a difference – a hilariously funny story of 15 year old Luke and his adventures among the badmen.

Last Stand
at
Goodbye Gulch

by
REX BENEDICT

HEINEMANN EDUCATIONAL BOOKS
LONDON

Heinemann Educational Books Ltd
LONDON EDINBURGH MELBOURNE AUCKLAND TORONTO
HONG KONG SINGAPORE KUALA LUMPUR NEW DELHI
NAIROBI JOHANNESBURG LUSAKA IBADAN
KINGSTON

ISBN O 435 12223 I

© 1974 by Rex Benedict
First published in Great Britain 1975 by
Hamish Hamilton Children's Books Limited
First published in the New Windmill Series 1977

Published by
Heinemann Educational Books Ltd
48 Charles Street, London W1X 8AH
Printed and bound in Great Britain by
Morrison & Gibb Ltd, London and Edinburgh

★ *Contents*

⋆ Author's Note

Careful readers will be quick to note that there has been some tinkering with geography in this novel. Some may even suspect that Goodbye Gulch—scene of much of the action—is actually a bit off the Oklahoma map, or maybe up in the air somewhere. The author wishes to assure them that the gulch is neither off the map nor in the air, but rather that it has been nudged eastward a few miles from its original, notorious location. This was not done to deprive the citizens of the Panhandle of any of the glories or beauties of their heritage. It was done to permit the author to rely on his more intimate knowledge of the terrain and its inhabitants—the terrain being his boyhood home and the inhabitants being his ancestors.

1 ★ The Music of Promises

When word trickled down across the Nescatunga River that old man Sheldon was near to dying and bad in need of medicine, Doc Barnes spun a little circle of tobacco juice around the hitching post in front of the Paradise Saloon and said, "That means whisky."

"Who's gonna pay for it?" asked Antoine the barber.

"That's not the problem," Doc said.

And Doc was right. Even I knew that. Antoine sure didn't know much about the unwritten law of the Territory. Almost anybody would pay for a dying man's medicine. It was like his last request. It had to be provided, no matter what the cost. Honor bound—that's the way you say it. The only trouble was, old man Sheldon lived up across the Nescatunga River in Goodbye Gulch, and dying men in Goodbye Gulch weren't supposed to make last requests, especially last requests for last drinks, which was the most solemn of all last requests. Goodbye Gulch was what folks called Outlaw Territory. That was to distinguish it from the rest of the Oklahoma Territory, and nobody ever went up there unless he was choosing between it and a jail.

1

"That's not the problem," Doc said again. "The problem is . . ." Then he paused to wrestle with the tobacco in his cheek.

Even before he said what I knew he was going to say, I began to hear the music—what you might call the music of promises. It was faint at first, but it grew stronger as I saw the prospects open up before me. And I knew when I heard the music exactly what I had to do. It's called "taking the bull by the horns." And I think I ought to say that if your name's Gore maybe you shouldn't go around doing that. Might lead to grief. Might even lead to your destruction prematurely. But of course if you're the kind that hears the music of promises, you won't even notice the untender hints of bloodshed suggested by your name. At least I didn't. I, Luke Gore, known to my admirers as Territory Gore, heard the music of promises and knew the time had come for me to take the bull by the horns. It didn't sound the least bit slaughterous.

To tell you the truth, it sounded beautiful. They were the exact right words for the occasion. First time it ever happened to me. The late Geoffrey Tolliver himself, my model in words and deeds, couldn't have done better. It was Geoffrey Tolliver who addicted me to such beauties of expression. He was United States Marshal for the Oklahoma Territory, quite a while since deceased. His words and deeds are still held in glorious memory along the Cimarron and Salt Fork Rivers, where he plied his trade. Known as the man who cleaned up the Territory. Pictures of him hang in every saloon. He's even mentioned in the history books. I never knew him. Before my time.

Saw his tombstone though. Just one word on it. GONE. Talk about a fittin' word. I always figured he chiseled it there himself, beforehand, though some folks say the chiseler was an old outlaw who couldn't contain his feelings or relief long enough to chisel out the rest, which was BUT NOT FORGOTTEN. Might be true, since the carving is off-center to the left, having a hasty look about it. Either way, the word fit, just like all his words and beautiful expressions. I found them in a book called *The Life & Times of Marshal Geoffrey Tolliver* by Anonymous.

I don't waste my time on bad men. It's the mean ones I'm after.

When it comes to fear, I practice total abstinence.

Duty is duty, no matter how much it hurts you.

Pay no attention to broken bones. They'll heal, one way or the other.

A man's reputation is sacred. Do not tamper with it.

I don't recall if the marshal ever said anything about taking the bull by the horns, but I imagine he did, otherwise it probably wouldn't have come so naturally to me. And that's the way it came, as natural as my own name, which, by the way, I got from him too. I mean Territory, of course. Comes from that expression of his about things goin' with the Territory, like the time he brought in that unholy gang of outlaws along with their stolen money and sat wounded on his horse in front of the Paradise Saloon—tobacco stains at the edges of his drooping mustache—and listened to the people of Bitter Wells marvel at what he had done single-handed at the risk of his life. According to Anonymous, he didn't pay much attention to them. Just dropped the sacks of money to the ground, wiped a little dried blood from off his arm, looked off toward the rimrocks in the distance, and said, "It goes with the Territory."

I use the words a lot—mostly in the wrong places—after reading that, and for my devotion to their beauty the name of Territory was hung upon me for the rest of my days.

The only words the marshal ever used that didn't fit were his deathbed words. According to Anonymous, they were, "Never go into Goodbye Gulch." For a man who practiced total abstinence from fear and expected the same from others, those words were a mystery. Like all the marshal's words, they were quoted near and far, and the mystery of their meaning grew. Folks argued about them as the years passed and kept away from Goodbye Gulch. The only man in living memory—actually the marshal was still alive at the time—who had ever gone into Goodbye Gulch was a tax collector. And that was the last anybody ever heard of him. So people went on arguing about the meaning of the words and keeping away from Goodbye Gulch right up to that moment when Doc finally got his tobacco straightened out and said, "The problem is, who's gonna deliver it?"

A little crowd had gathered, and everyone had an opinion.

"It's a job for the sheriff," Mayor Bicker said, "or the deputy."

"Sheriff's got blackleg," Doc said. "The deputy's dead drunk. He ain't the right man to deliver whisky anyway."

"He ain't the right man for anything," said Will Jinks the undertaker. "I think I'll lay him out someday when he's a-boozin'."

"Do not condemn him for his mortal weaknesses," said Reverend Bonely Scraggs. "Which of us does not possess them?"

I could vouch for that. Bitter Wells probably had as many mortal weaknesses as there were mortals in the town. Everybody was addicted to something. If it wasn't legendary lawmen and beautiful expressions, like me, it was drink, like the deputy, or blackleg, like the sheriff. And if it wasn't drink or blackleg, it was money, like the banker. And if it wasn't money, it was horses, like old Wayward Bones, the Osage who ran the livery barn. And if it wasn't horses, it was something else, religion maybe, like Reverend Bonely Scraggs. Right now—you could see—it was the value of their lives. The slightest mention of Goodbye Gulch had a way of bringing out that addiction. They remembered the tax collector and the marshal's dying words.

"Well, now," said the mayor, "how bad is the sheriff?"

"Awful bad," Doc said. "And he'll get worse if he hears he has to go to the gulch. May even get hoof-and-mouth disease. He's been known to."

"Do not condemn him for his frailties," said Reverend Bonely Scraggs. "Which of us. . . ."

"How drunk is the deputy?" the mayor interrupted.

" 'Bout as usual," Antoine said. "I think he got into a keg of my bay rum."

5

"Well, now," the mayor said, "that leaves . . . let's see . . . hmmmm."

He knew who that left. That left—besides me and a couple of curious Indians, marveling endlessly at the white man's ways—him and the preacher and the doctor and the barber and the undertaker. All of them—except me and the Indians—seemed to be looking at the sky or up the street or at least somewhere else. Actually I guess you couldn't much blame them. Doc Barnes was too old. Mayor Bicker was too important. Reverend Bonely Scraggs was too saintly. Will Jinks was too clean. The sheriff was too sick. And the deputy of course was too drunk. Mortal weaknesses? I tell you, we got 'em. Don't know what it is. Must be the climate.

And so, while they looked at distant things and maybe hoped the problem would vanish in the air, I waited, in my mind the picture of a legendary marshal riding out alone, on my lips the beauty of the words that I would speak. And finally I spoke them, clean and clear.

"Gimme a horse. I'll deliver the whisky."

Beautiful words. Fittin' words. The music of promises fulfilled.

2 * Bullet Proof

As the marshal once said, "Keep one eye on your enemies and both eyes on your friends." He was right as usual, judging by what happened next. By which I mean, my friends started right off arranging things, supplying me with everything I needed and a lot of things I didn't, just as soon, that is, as they recovered from their surprise and delight and maybe their relief at finding a volunteer in their midst. Doc Barnes said, "I'll get the medicine." Mayor Bicker said, "I'll supply the horse." Will Jinks the undertaker said, "I'll furnish the shroud, in case you arrive too late." And Reverend Bonely Scraggs said, "If old man Sheldon has gone to his reward, put up a little marker and gather him some wild flowers from the fields of the Lord."

"Yes, and you better take a spade," said Antoine.

"And a hymnbook," added Reverend Scraggs. "I'll mark the proper songs. He was an old prospector, I believe."

I knew the proper songs, even those for old prospectors. And I knew something else too. They were rushing me. To add to the confusion, Sheriff Boggs limped out of the jail and started protesting to the mayor that I couldn't go because I was too young, and if I got killed, which he said was likely, he would get in trouble with the circuit judge for contributing to the delinquency of a minor.

"Hogwash, Boggs," the mayor said. "If he"—meanin' me—"gets killed, I'll personally take the responsibility."

Now there's the kind of man to keep both eyes on.

Sheriff Boggs limped back inside the jail. Mayor Bicker went on giving orders, which he very much liked to do. "Get the supplies," he said. "A man is dying up there in that . . ." He didn't finish it, but Reverend Scraggs did. ". . . God forsaken place."

Everybody rushed off in different directions, rounding up the shrouds and spades and hymnbooks and whisky needed for the mission. You could tell they were afraid I might change my mind.

They needn't have worried. The words were spoken, and now they had to be lived up to. That was as much a part of the Territory as anything else. If you valued your reputation, you didn't speak words you couldn't live up to, no matter how beautiful they were. And if you valued your life, you took that into consideration too, despite the music in your head. The marshal said it best. "Don't bite off more than you can chew." I think he was addressing the Dalton Gang just before they rode out on that mission to Coffeyville, Kansas, and ended up dead on a hayrack. Sounds like that was the occasion anyway.

I didn't like to think I had anything in common with the Dalton Gang, least of all the way they ended up. The Dalton Gang hadn't exactly been on a mission of mercy. More interested in the Coffeyville bank.

8

Still, just like Bob Dalton, I had gone against the marshal's advice. "Never go into Goodbye Gulch." He had been very plain about it. That worried me a little, since it was common knowledge that he had never in his life given bad advice to anyone, not even to Dick Yeager, an outlaw he didn't much care for. I guess I ought to say especially to Dick Yeager, like that time in front of the Paradise Saloon when he had advised Dick Yeager not to reach for his guns. Now that had been very sound advice. But since the marshal's words about goin' into the gulch were deathbed words and most unfittin' to his character—makin' no sense at all—I took care of my worries by telling myself that he had probably been, as they say, delirious at the time. No other explanation for it Couldn't have been fear. He practiced total abstinence from fear. Said so himself. Wasn't delirious when he said it either. In the prime of life. Around eighty-three. Died at ninety-six, covered with glory.

I hadn't yet made it to sixteen. Didn't even yet know if I could practice total abstinence from fear or anything else.

"Here's the medicine," Doc Barnes said, luggin' up the bottles.

"Here's the shroud," said Will Jinks.

"Here's the hymnbook and the spade," said Reverend Scraggs.

"And here's the horse," said Wayward Bones, the old Osage who ran the livery barn. "Name's Bullet Proof."

I stepped back. You just naturally stepped back in front of a horse like that. I couldn't keep from wondering where Wayward Bones had got him on such short notice.

Probably had been keeping him in hiding for some extra special occasion like this. He was a lean gray gelding with an unkindly glint in his eye. Didn't seem to like me much. Wouldn't let Doc get close to him with the whisky. Kept his head high, the glint shining, as if looking for someone worthy of being stomped to death.

"Is he broke?" I asked.

"Almost," Wayward Bones said. Old Bones was fairly struttin' with pride at the wild and magnificent animal he had chosen for me. "By the time you get back, he'll be broke. And if there's a horse that can get you back, it's this one." He made it sound like the chances weren't very good and that it depended entirely on the horse.

I didn't like that murderous glint in his eye.

"That's for his enemies," Bones said, seeing my distrust. "Let him get your smell. Take him by the nose and twitch him until he lowers his head."

I got a hold of his nose, at the risk of my life, and started twitchin' him.

"Hold him that way for a minute," Bones said. "It's the Comanche way of breedin' devotion."

"I'm not a Comanche," I said, keeping one eye on those deadly hoofs.

"Neither am I," Bones said. "But the horse doesn't know that."

It was a pretty slobbery way of breedin' devotion, and I got knocked around a little, but Bullet Proof finally relaxed and quit trying to swing me over his head.

"That's good," Bones said. "Now you smell as sweet to him as prairie hay."

"How can you tell?"

"See it in his eye."

He still had that unkindly glint in his eye, but I figured Bones was right and that the glint was for his enemies. Just hoped he kept them straight. Sure didn't want any trouble with a horse, especially a horse like that. Had enough troubles as it was.

I was in the saddle then, along with my gear, kind of feelin' for tremors of friendship from the horse, when Clyde Blood rose up from behind a wagon and came across the street. Clyde Blood, pure Osage, was always rising up out of somewhere—or more exactly out of nowhere—and coming silently into my life, bringing with him favors of friendship that usually turned out to be disasters of the worst kind. Been doin' it all his life . . . all our lives, since we were the same age and had grown up together. I never had got used to it. Every time he did it, it meant trouble of some kind. Maybe not right then, but it still meant trouble. I think he could sniff trouble, even future trouble. He meant well, and we were good friends, but that didn't mean his favors weren't omens of disaster. That must have come from having generations of medicine men for ancestors.

He handed me a small packet of what looked like herbs and a box of kitchen matches. Bullet Proof didn't seem to mind his presence, both of them being Osage.

"Keep 'em dry," he said, which was his way of saying that I would not only need herbs for medicine and matches for smoke signals of distress but that I would probably die of my wounds without the first and old age without the second, it taking me that long to strike a fire from twigs.

You *never* know what's in an Osage's head. Young or old. They seem to know what's going to happen before

11

it happens. That beautiful, mean horse. He was not chosen carelessly. He was—to Wayward Bones—as much a part of that mission as I was. And those herbs and that box of kitchen matches. They weren't just handed out as idle gifts. They were meant to serve some purpose, though what it was I wouldn't know until the time came. And then just as I was riding out, to cheers and applause from a grateful mayor and his friends, along with protests from the sheriff, old Wayward Bones blocked my path and lifted his long right arm, as if of a mind to parley with some ancient general of the army, saying in a high sing-song, "There is something I must tell you, O Territory Gore."

Then he waited . . . for me. I knew how much importance he attached to ceremony, so I lifted my voice, though not my arm, and said in a high singsong, "What is it, O Wayward Bones?"

Then he, in high singsong, said, "Cross over the river before the storm hits, O Territory Gore."

There wasn't a cloud in the sky.

"What storm, O Wayward Bones?"

Now the rest of the ceremony was up to him, the wise and ancient chief, dispensing ancient wisdom. Majestically he lowered his arm—grown a little flabby with age—and assumed a stance of solemn dignity not often seen in front of the Paradise Saloon. Sniffing a little, looking far into the west where the rimrocks stood, he said, "The tornado, O Territory Gore. You can feel it in the air."

I tell you, you *never* know. Still, it *was* a nice little ceremony. Just the right thing to get me started off wrong.

3 * Crossing the Nescatunga

To be truthful, I had a feeling I was headed for disaster.
Like old Wayward Bones, I could feel it in the air. It was
late on a hot afternoon in June and that southwest wind
had something sullen and foreboding in it. It seemed to
be making dark and threatening promises which, along
about nightfall, it would keep. That's the time they usually hit, and that's the direction they always come from
... tornadoes, I mean.

"Cross over the river before the storm hits, O Territory
Gore." Wayward Bones hadn't said anything about getting back across the river. Just like an Osage, to leave out
the most important part. And it was for sure the most important part, because if that storm hit while I was on the
other side and that river rose in back of me, there wouldn't
be any getting back for a while.

That glint-eyed horse of mine was feeling something
too. But then I knew that Osage horses are just like their
masters. They feel all sorts of things that don't register
on ordinary mortals until it's too late. Also I had a feeling
that horse mistrusted me just as much as I mistrusted him.
You could tell it from the way he occasionally tried to

slip out from under me after first bouncing me a little higher in the air than necessary. Wayward Bones had said he was almost broke, which meant that he was just as close to being wild as he was to being tame. Also he kept trying to show me how fast he could run, if I would just let him.

I held him in, kind of takin' his word for it. Then, just as we were getting into the red shale canyons leading to the river, I saw what he had been sniffing on the wind. About a mile away, coming out of what was now an almost obscured sun, was another rider. He seemed to be converging with me at Dead Horse Crossing, which after you cross you're in Goodbye Gulch. Ridin' hard too, like maybe tryin' to beat me there or cut me off. Old Bullet Proof sensed the same thing. He started pullin' at the bit and snortin' like a horse that knows when he's been challenged. I let him go, figuring that wouldn't hurt our friendship any, knowing as I did that nothing pleases an Osage horse—or an Osage either—as much as winning a race. I think it's in the blood.

The race was on then, and Bullet Proof was in command. He wasn't running full speed, just hammering along at what you might call a terrifying clip, considering the terrain we were crossing. One misstep would have sent us both thundering to destruction. That glint in his eye must have been terrifying too, though now I couldn't see it for the wind in my face. Gradually he was picking up more speed. Seemed to be a slow starter. It looked like it was going to be a close race. Both horses were coming down the last quarter mile now, and the canyons were behind us. That's when Bullet Proof finally laid it on, all of it. And for just a second I couldn't believe it. Never saw anything like it. That horse had been loafing. He thundered up to Dead Horse Crossing a full forty yards ahead of the other horse. It was all I could do to keep him from crashing right on through the canebrakes and into the river.

Behind me the other horse stopped, and in my head were the marshal's words, "Never turn your back on a stranger." It was a little late for that. I had won the race, but my back was to the stranger. Turning Bullet Proof around, slow and easy like you're supposed to in such moments, I expected to see the barrel of a gun and hear some hardened hombre say, "Don't reach for anything. 'Twouldn't be taken kindly." Instead I saw with sweet surprise a flash of red lips and brown eyes beneath a Stetson hat, and in my mind I heard the words, "She must be a Cherokee. Too pretty for anything else."

"Howdy," she said.

"Howdy."

She sat that nervous, blowing horse as if she had been born there. And I guessed maybe she had, because she was already saying something to me, and I could tell by her words that she—like the rimrocks and the water holes—went with the Territory.

"Name's Cherokee Waters," she said. "I've got business on the other side of the river."

"Territory Gore," I said. But in my mind, defenseless against all beautiful expressions, I was thinking that you wouldn't even need a guitar if you were to sing a song called Cherokee Waters. The words were all you needed. Music a-plenty. The chords would just get in the way.

15

All you had to do was just wail it a little, stretch out the words and make them say:

> Cherokee Waters
> Cherokee Waters
> Youngest, fairest
> Of Santoo's daughters . . .

Who Santoo was, I didn't know. It didn't matter. He seemed to fit. One thing was certain. He had named his daughter well. *Cherokee Waters . . . Cherokee Waters . . . Youngest . . . fairest of Santoo's daughters.* Even Bullet Proof, an Osage, lifted his head and snorted softly.

"Got business on the other side of the river," she said again, as if I hadn't heard or hadn't understood. And then, as if I had asked her what her business was, which I hadn't because that wasn't done too freely in those parts, she said, "Got to clear my daddy's name. Need a confession from a dyin' man. A dyin' man's confession will pass for legal, if," she added, "it's in ink. Least that's what Judge Docker says. He's the judge at Rimrock City." Then real quickly, "What do you think?"

I didn't know what to think. Keeping on safe ground, I said, "Everybody's got a right to his opinion, especially a judge."

"That's what I figure," she said. "He's sure a good one."

"Judge Docker?"

"No. Your horse."

Cherokee Waters . . . Cherokee Waters . . . Youngest . . . fairest of Santoo's daughters. I guessed the beauty of the words was working on me, because I was having trouble understanding.

16

"Osage, isn't he?" she asked.

"If you mean the horse, yes. If you mean the judge, I don't know."

"I mean the horse. Judge Docker is a Choctaw. Anyway, he says a dyin' man's confession is proper and legal and binding and will clear my daddy's name." She took a deep breath and said very firmly, " 'Cause my daddy didn't shoot the tax collector, like the vicious tongues say. I aim to clear all that up. All I need's a signature or a mark, whichever is easier for the dyin' man. I may have to guide his hand. Judge Docker says I can't use any duress though, which is all right with me, 'cause I don't know what it is and he didn't say. What do you think?"

She sure liked to get opinions on the law.

"It's deathbed persuasion," I said, using the marshal's definition. "Means you can't be too rough when you guide the dyin' man's hand."

"That's what I figured," she said. And then, "I aim to be gentle. I've got this big fountain pen and this piece of paper. Judge Docker gave them to me." She held up the biggest fountain pen I had ever seen. It must have held a gallon of ink. As she put it away, she said, "You look all right to me, Territory Gore, otherwise I wouldn't be telling you all of this. Mostly I judge men by their horses." Without even pausing, she looked around her and said, "We're gonna have a tornado. You can feel it."

Nowhere in Marshal Tolliver's book had he set forth any rules for dealing with women you met on the trail. That was because the marshal had, generally speaking, kept away from women, worshiping only the law. Come to think of it, he had once said it—on page 82, I think—"The law is my mistress," the way Jim Bowie referred to

17

his knife, and Wyatt Earp to his long-barreled pistol.

I had moved out of Cherokee's way but she didn't seem in any hurry to cross the river. I knew she was waiting for me to tell her where I was headed, and I also knew she wouldn't ask, since that would be bad manners. I figured that the dyin' man she sought was old man Sheldon, and I couldn't keep from wondering how she would feel if the whisky I was taking to him saved his life. I guessed she wouldn't mind, so long as she got her confession and cleared her daddy's name.

"How'd you hear about the dyin' man?" I asked.

She smiled, a bright flash of secrecy and mystery, mixed, I thought, with just a tender touch of sorrow for my innocence. "From the Indians, of course."

Of course. Didn't they usually know everything that was going on, even before it happened? She was still smiling when I said, "I'll see you across the river, Cherokee Waters." And as I pronounced those two beautiful words, I wished I had a drooping mustache with tobacco stains around the edge.

"I figured you would," she said.

Dusk was just falling when we started across the almost dry river bed. This was the river where, according to legend, Coronado and his conquistadors had lost faith and turned back, saying goodbye to their dreams of golden cities. Around us a heavy silence hung. It seemed the calm before the storm . . . in more ways than one. But I figured if we hurried we could still make it in and out before the storm broke and the river rose to cut us off. All we had to do was find old man Sheldon's diggin's, that upturned plot of earth where he, like the conquistadors, had spent his life searching for gold. Once there, I could hold up his dyin' head long enough for Cherokee Waters to guide his dyin' hand in making the mark that would clear her daddy's name. And then . . . well, then I just hoped the medicine did its work and saved his life. The extreme merciful act of digging a grave in Goodbye Gulch didn't much appeal to me, especially on a night when a storm was brewing and the man you were burying was rumored to have a fortune in hidden gold. Men had been shot for being merciful like that.

I didn't know how Cherokee Waters felt about it, but I figured that this was as good a time as any to start practicing total abstinence from fear.

4 · Black Funnels

I was ready . . . for anything. Except what came. Seems I'm a little plagued that way. And I've got to say that if you want to keep alive out in that wild region of rimrocks and sudden storms you'd better put your faith in women, Osages, and horses. They always know—I don't know how—when a tornado is going to hit. And as far as I know, they are the only ones that do know.

Every one of them had told me, in their way, and I hadn't paid much attention to their warnings, knowing as I did that nobody can predict when and where a tornado will hit. Then it hit, just as we were going up the river bank into the gulch—two big black funnels, behind us, twisting and bending against the sky, out of the southwest.

There was a quick wind change, the sound of cracking trees, the sting of sand against the face, and Bullet Proof took off—northeast, naturally. That horse knew instinctively which way to run. I couldn't see that wild glint in his eye, but I knew it was there. I couldn't see Cherokee Waters either, but I could hear her horse crashing through the brush behind me. The wind, violent and straight, was bending everything to earth. There were more trees along that river bank than I had expected, big cottonwoods with low-hanging limbs. At the speed we were going I didn't dare look around, for fear of getting my head knocked off by a branch. Also I didn't like to think of what the lightning would do if it struck anywhere near the tops of those trees. They bring it down to earth in a fierce way. No worse place to be. Bullet Proof seemed to sense that too. He was running almost full speed now, doing his best to get us out of there. Every time it thundered and the lightning flashed, he laid his ears back a little more and pounded the earth a little harder. My affection for him was growing fast, and maybe Wayward Bones was right about him being the horse that could get us back if any horse could. Cherokee's horse stayed right behind us, as if puttin' his faith in Bullet Proof too. When we finally broke out into low thickets of wild sand plums, I pulled up on a knoll and we looked back down toward the river. It was—no other word for it—terrifyin'. No matter how many times you see them, they're always terrifyin'. Between the lightning flashes you could see two raging black funnels—big at the top—twisting up into the sky, dipping down and lifting up, then weaving in against each other, then dropping down again, and always moving generally northeast. The two funnels were cutting what looked like a leisurely, almost playful, swathe of destruction as they moved over the land.

Suddenly the bushes around us stood still, so quickly and so still that it seemed the world and everything in it was holding its breath. I realized then—too late it seemed to me—that we were caught in the edge of the raging funnels. It was the quietest quiet I had ever heard, and somewhere out beyond the quietness was the raging thunder. Seemed to come from another world.

"It's the calm," Cherokee shouted. "We're in the edge of it." Her voice seemed to carry clear around the world.

Bullet Proof was going crazy now, rearing, fighting to go, to get out of there, wiser than the human holding him. Every nerve and muscle in his body was trembling. He knew we were almost caught. He knew what was coming next—total disaster for humans and horses. Nature was out to get them both.

"Hold on!" I shouted to Cherokee. "I'm turning him loose!"

The last fading words I heard were, "I figure . . . that's the . . . best . . . thing . . . to . . . do . . ." as Bullet Proof lunged, seemed to lift, then swept us into the night. He had full rein.

That horse—that wonderful horse, I ought to say—may have had some special Osage charm against bullets, but he knew and I knew that he had no such charms against tornadoes. For that he would have to rely on his instincts and his speed. I just hoped he had some special charm against gopher holes and canyon rims and other invisible perils. He was running through that black and raging night with no regard for perils of any kind. Perhaps his nose sniffed them, but it had to sniff fast and sure at that speed. Once or twice I felt him veer, gently like a leaping cat, as if gliding over some unseen danger, and I hoped Cherokee's horse veered with him. I had just put that thought out of my mind when another fearful possibility occurred to me—barbed wire. Barbed wire had practically circled the

22

earth, and there was no reason to think that Goodbye Gulch didn't have its share. At that speed, in that blackness, no horse could have seen it in time. What that would do wasn't pretty to think about. I had seen what horses look like after hitting four strands of barb wire at full speed. In my head the words stayed, fearful words that wouldn't wish away. Four strands, I kept thinking. Four strands of tight barbed wire singing in the black wind.

That was when I first noticed that we were out of the calm and back in the raging wind again. I glanced around. Cherokee Waters—girl of the beautiful name—was still there, and crazily I thought, "Perhaps she has a touch of Comanche, for no Cherokee could ride like that." Whatever her touches, she was still there. And so were the black funnels—gruesome, beautiful, threatening things, their twisting bodies lit by lightning flashes. One thing was certain. Even if we lived, we were going to be in Goodbye Gulch a while. That storm would bring a deluge with it. By morning the Nescatunga would be overflowing. Dead Horse Crossing, the only crossing in those parts, would not even be visible.

It was about then that I felt Bullet Proof veer on the wind again and not veer back. He was changing his direction, turning slightly to the north. I couldn't keep from wondering, "How does he know? What does he sniff?" We were in mostly sand hill country now with only an occasional tree or clump of bending sumac bushes. Behind me the other horse veered too. I was still wondering how strange it was that horses should know where safety lies and men should not, knowing even as I wondered that it really wasn't anything to marvel about. I had learned

23

long ago never to question the instincts of a horse, especially when he's running for his life or the life of his rider. You don't ask questions then; you just hang on. And while you hang, you question the wisdom of the Lord for inventing gopher holes and the foolishness of men for inventing barbed wire.

We dropped gradually off the sand hills then and down a hard-packed slope, still at that same speed. The slope led into a narrow canyon about a hundred yards long. There Bullet Proof stopped so fast that the spade and the whisky slammed up against my back, and Cherokee's horse almost crashed into us. There right in front of us was an opening dug straight into the side of a hill, big enough to drive a wagon into. Heavy timbers served as beams for the ceiling. All around lay mounds of earth piled high. From inside came what looked like light from a lantern.

Bullet Proof sniffed once, stuck his head inside and kept on walking. Cherokee's horse followed. For a moment it was a different kind of calm, the quiet calm of safety, refuge, a feeling that horses and humans had won and nature had lost.

But only for a moment.

There beside the lantern, sitting on what looked like a keg of gunpowder, was a man—big, old, bushy-whiskered —holding a shotgun across his knees. Shifting the gun just slightly—actually kind of politely—in our direction, he said, "Howdy. Name's Sheldon. Welcome to my diggin's." Then he kind of leaned over easy and laid his head on the hammers of the shotgun, as if he had decided to take a little nap.

24

"That gun's loaded," Cherokee said.

"Both barrels," I said.

"Looks like he's dyin', all right," she said. "How do you revive a dyin' man?"

"There's lots of ways," I said.

But I didn't even have time to reach for the whisky in my saddlebags, because right then the lantern guttered and the flame died. We were in the eye of the tornado ... no air.

"Sit very still on your horse," I said. "This mine is filled with dynamite, and I figure his finger is on the trigger."

"I figure you're right," she said.

5 ∗ A Stubborn Trigger Finger

So there we sat, tornadoes outside, dynamite inside, and a dyin' man's finger curlin' round the trigger of a shotgun.

"They say," Cherokee said, "that as the finger grows cold it tightens up."

"So I've heard."

"How long does it take?"

"Don't rightly know. It's not the kind of thing you run into every day."

"What do we do?"

I was spared from answering that and thankful for it—there not being any answer—for right then those tornadoes hit that hill with force enough to shake a dead man out of his grave. Those funnels must have been passing directly over us. The old timbers creaked and the hill seemed to want to lift right into the air. Dirt came spilling down from the rafters, and the horses began to get nervous. Through the mazes of the mine a powerful wind shook and rattled everything. Objects crashed against the walls and rolled under our horses' feet. I kept waiting for the explosion from a keg of dynamite or a shotgun or both. Seemed kind of crazy that you could escape from a tornado only to find your life hangin' on the temperature of a dead man's finger. Crazy or not, that was the way it was. The timbers groaned. Dust fell. The hill made what felt like one last attempt to fly, shuddered, settled down, and I knew the worst was over. From outside you could hear the wind blowing clean and the rain falling hard. The tornado was gone . . . but the shotgun wasn't.

"What do you think?" Cherokee asked.

That must have been her favorite expression, and it sure covered a lot of territory.

"We're still alive," I said, not wanting her to lose faith in me, "but I can't promise you anything."

"How are you fixed for matches?"

"Got plenty of them," I said, seeing Clyde Blood's face, hearing Clyde Blood's voice, and wondering as usual what had been in Clyde Blood's head. "They're in my saddlebags with the whisky."

"You oughtn't to drink," she said. "It's sinful."

"It's for emergencies. Steady your horse."

The match flared. The horses started, then settled down.

"He's still there," she said. "So is the lantern."

"So is the shotgun. Here." I gave her the box of matches, keeping three for myself. Then I got off Bullet Proof, taking care not to drop the burnt-out match too soon. I had a feeling there was gunpowder sprinkled all over the floor. "Light one of them real easy," I said. "Don't want any flarin' match heads spittin' through the air."

She lit it, real easy.

"It's on the other side of him," she said.

27

"I know." She was talking about the lantern. I had either to go over him and the keg of gunpowder or in front of the shotgun to get to the lantern. Either way looked like suicide to me. Her match went out.

"Light another one," I said. "Real easy. And keep on talkin'. As long as you're talkin', I'll know I'm alive. Doesn't matter what you say. Just keep on talkin'."

That for her was easy. I had a feeling that if that gun went off and the explosion went off too, she would still be talkin'. I even fancied I could hear her saying, during the explosion, "The way I figure it . . ." And I was right. There wasn't any explosion, but now she was saying, "The way I figure it, you might as well walk in front of the shotgun, 'cause if it goes off it won't do any more damage to either of us than that keg of dyna . . ." where I stopped listening to the words and just listened to the sounds of a human voice. And the voice went on, even and calm. It went on while her match went out and she lit another one and I walked in front of the shotgun and lit the lantern. It even went on—me still not listening to the words—while I knelt and tenderly laid my finger tip against old man Sheldon's trigger finger tip and started easing off the pressure. That was when I noticed something. "He's alive," I said.

"Did you hear him breathing?"

"No. I heard him grunt."

Then I noticed something else. Dead or alive—it didn't seem to make much difference—that hand was wrapped like a claw around the gun. "It won't uncurl," I said.

She was off her horse then and kneeling on the other side of the shotgun. We must have looked like two innocents at prayer, which in a sense I guess we were. "You're right," she said. "Looks like it's grown that way."

"Comes from sleepin' with your finger on the trigger all your life, I guess."

"He grunted again."

"I heard."

"What do you think?"

Her favorite expression.

"Get me the whisky. No, wait!" I had forgotten about Bullet Proof's unnatural mistrust of all mortals that hadn't been properly presented to him. "You hold his finger off the trigger. I'll get the whisky."

She put her finger tip against the stubborn claw, and I made another trip around the shotgun to the saddle-bags, then back again with the bottle.

"Why do you carry the whisky if you don't drink?" she asked. "Bootleggin'?"

"Just hold the finger."

His head was still down and his mouth was lost in the whiskers, so I just poured at him mostly, rubbin' it into the whiskers as I went. Soaked him good.

"He's gruntin' again," she said.

"Keep holdin' the finger. He may jerk up hard when he smells the spirits."

"Smells nasty," she said.

"Not to a dyin' man."

"What's that sloppin' sound?"

"He's lickin' the booze."

"His finger's relaxing a little."

"Try to push it through the trigger guard. If you can get it to curve a little, I can get hold of the knuckle joint."

We were still kneeling, the gun between us. Behind her the horses stood, noses forward expectantly, intrigued, it seemed to me, at the mysterious works and ways of humans. She got the finger to curve a little, and I got a grip on the knuckle. A finger joint cracked a little as I bent it outward and eased it up against the side of the barrel. It kind of whacked into place there, the callouses making a little rasping sound against the metal.

"I'll hold the finger," I said. "You lift his head real slowly."

"By the whiskers?"

"By whatever you can get a hold of."

She lifted his head slowly, partly by the hair and partly by the whiskers and partly by his hat too, there being no sure way to know where one started and the other stopped. Then I bent over the gun and carefully eased the hammers forward one at a time. Old man Sheldon wasn't disarmed, but at least the gun was uncocked and the finger was detriggered.

"I figured you could do it," Cherokee said.

"We're not finished yet. We've got to revive him. I'll hold his head up while you pour some more whisky down him."

"How do I do it?"

"His mouth's open. Just pour it in."

"Won't it gag him?"

"That's better than dyin'. Pour."

"It's sinful," she said. But she poured.

"Now watch his eyes shine."

"They're closed."

"They'll open."

They did. Old man Sheldon blinked a couple of times and then his eyes lit up in the lantern light.

"You all right, Mr. Sheldon?" Cherokee asked.

"Don't rightly know," he said. His voice sounded healthy enough. "My finger feels funny. Don't feel right. Like it was out of place or somethin'." He squinted along the gun. Didn't seem to see too good. Probably shot at everything that moved. Then he saw his finger. "What's it doin' out there? Supposed to be on the trigger. It'll take me all day to get that finger back in place again. Got what's called shotgun cramp." Then he seemed to forget about the finger and said real pleasantly, "You young folks runnin' from the law?" He made it sound like it was the most natural thing in the world to be doin', maybe the only thing in the world to be doin'. Seemed to excite him just to think about it.

"No, sir," Cherokee said. "We're respectable."

"Hee! Hee! With a horse like that," he said, squintin' up at Bullet Proof, "you could afford to be disrespectable. The law never would catch up with you, at least not until the horse got old. Wouldn't want him for an enemy though. Osage. I can tell. Nobody else except maybe a Comanche could put a glint like that in a horse's eye." He belched big and said, "Wish he wouldn't do *that* though, not in here."

I hadn't noticed what Bullet Proof was doin', until it was too late and he had already done it, just lowerin' his tail.

"The gun makes him nervous," I said.

"We didn't come here to talk about horses," Cherokee said.

"Hee! Hee! Betcha didn't," old man Sheldon said, belchin' again pleasantly and tryin' to work his stiff finger back to its proper place on the trigger. "Not if you're runnin' from the law. Hee! Hee!" How he liked the idea.

"We're not runnin' from the law," Cherokee said.

"Ah," he said, belching sadly. That seemed to take the joy out of things, that and the finger, which still wouldn't uncurl. "What's your name, young lady? That is if you don't mind tellin' me. You might also help me get my finger straightened out. Joint doesn't seem to work right."

"Name's Cherokee Waters," Cherokee said. "And I will gladly help you with your finger, 'cause I've got a paper for you to sign."

"Oh, my!" he said, as if though he could deal with dynamite and gunpowder, he could never deal with something like a piece of paper. "That's apt to be a problem. Doubt if I can hold a pencil. Can't write anyway. And I think my finger must be broke at the joint. What's your name, young fellow?" You could tell he didn't want to talk about signing any paper.

"Gore," I said. "Territory Gore."

He winked at me, as if to say that it was as good a name as any for a man runnin' from the law. Then he said, "How'd that finger get out there anyway?"

"It was on the trigger," Cherokee said.

"That's where a trigger finger's supposed to be."

"Would you like another drink?" I asked.

"Sure would."

It only took two long pulls—much appreciated I

could tell—to relax his trigger finger and, at the same time, finish off the bottle. Before he could get the trigger finger back in its proper place, Cherokee laid a sheet of paper across the hammers of the shotgun and held out the fountain pen.

He squinted at it. "Why you pointin' a gun at me?"

"It's a fountain pen," Cherokee said.

"Looks like a gun. It's as big as a gun." He was right. Even to a man with good eyes it would have looked like a gun, especially if it was pointed at you.

"Here's the confession," Cherokee said, tapping the paper on the hammers of the shotgun.

For a moment he looked down at it, not even squintin', not even trying to see. Then he shook his head sadly, his whiskers scraping across the paper, and said, "Can't hold the pen. My finger won't wrap around it. Can't write anyway. Can't even read. Can't sign what I can't read."

He was right about the pen. That finger wouldn't curl around anything that wasn't shaped like a trigger.

"I'll guide your hand," Cherokee said. "You can make your mark. Territory will be the witness."

"What does it say?"

"It says you know who shot the tax collector and will name him."

"Oh, my!" he said, as if though he might forget a lot of things, he would never forget that tax collector or the man who shot him. It seemed to be of great importance. He belched again and said, "Can't do that, ma'am."

"Why not?"

"Took an oath. Gave my word. That makes it sacred. Got to carry the secret with me to the grave." Then he added, "Maybe before I die I'll change my mind. Depends on how I feel at the time."

"We heard you were dyin'," Cherokee said. "That's why I came."

"That was a trick," he said.

I noticed he didn't laugh. "Would you like another drink?" I asked.

"Sure would."

But Cherokee said no. "You're revived enough, Mr. Sheldon."

He didn't seem to mind. Just belched pleasantly and said, "Sure a nice horse you got there." And then, leaning a little forward, "Can't tell you about the tax collector, much as I would like to. But I can tell you a few other things more important yet."

We waited.

He hesitated. Then he motioned for us to lean down close across the shotgun. When our hat brims were all touching and the reek of whisky was riotous in the air, he whispered, "You're in terrible trouble, both of you. They'll catch you before the sun comes up."

"Who'll catch us?" I asked.

"Dick Creel mainly," he whispered. "Dick Creel and his gang of old marshals. There's others too. Tom Beasley and his gang of old outlaws. Maybe they'll even gang up on you if they think there's any money in it. But it's Dick Creel to watch out for. He's the one that put out the message. 'Bout me dyin', I mean. It was a trap, not made for you, but you fell into it. Take my advice and head for Kansas. And if they catch you before you get there, tell 'em you're runnin' from the law. They understand that. Run," he said, "and don't look back. Run like you were runnin' from the law."

That was all he said. Didn't utter another sound, except to belch. Just laid his head back down on the hammers of the shotgun and started snorin' softly.

"Is he dyin'?" Cherokee asked.

"No. Dyin' men don't belch that hard. He's just old and tired and pleasantly drunk. But that's all he's gonna tell us and he's even gonna forget he told us that much."

"His finger's back on the trigger," she said. And then, "Who's Dick Creel?"

"He's an outlaw. Used to be a U.S. marshal. Read about him in a book once. Went bad."

"Like Bob Dalton?"

"More or less, except Dick Creel lived longer."

"They used to do that a lot, didn't they? Change occupations, I mean."

I wanted to tell her that there was an exception in the history of the West and that his name was Marshal Geoffrey Tolliver, that he was born a lawman, lived a lawman's life and died a lawman's death, faithful to the end . . . to use his own words. But there wasn't time for that.

"He sure belches, doesn't he?" she said. "Did you notice how the shotgun goes up and down every time he does it?"

I noticed. And walking around that shotgun for what I hoped was the last time, I said, "Let's go."

"What about the confession?"

"The game's changed. It's no longer a case of reviving or burying a dead man—'cause he's not dyin'—or clearing anybody's name. The stakes are higher." I was pleased despite myself to hear the words fit so well. "If we get caught here in this cave or even in that narrow canyon outside, we'll never get out. Doesn't do much good to have good horses if there's no place to run."

"Reckon you're right."

We were in the saddle then and riding out, lowering our heads so as not to hit the beams. Behind us old man Sheldon was asleep on the gunpowder keg, snorin' and belchin', the barrel of the shotgun goin' up and down.

6 ★ Grunt

To use one of Marshal Tolliver's favorite expressions, we jumped from the fryin' pan into the fire. It's bad enough to be in the presence of a friendly shotgun aimed at a keg of dynamite, but it's worse to be in the presence of a forty-five aimed at you.

It didn't take me entirely by surprise. Old man Sheldon's warning had put me on my guard. Also Bullet Proof was trying to tell me something. We hadn't gone forty yards up that narrow canyon leading out from the mine before that horse sensed the presence of something he didn't like. Got real nervous. Kept tossing his head and snorting, seeming even meaner than usual. He didn't like it and I didn't like it, but that was the only way out.

"What's the matter with him?" Cherokee asked. Her horse, untrained by Osage hands, was walking along calmly in the dark.

"Something up ahead. Stay close behind me."

Then we saw it rise up out of the moonlight—first the hat, then the gun, then the figure dark against the sky. Behind him stood a horse, the reins hanging.

"Hold it ... there," he said. He was about ten feet

away, directly ahead. "Lift your hands . . . high." There was something strange about his voice. Didn't sound quite right. Seemed to grunt in between words, like he had about half swallowed his tongue or something.

"Stranger," I said, fighting against Bullet Proof, "I understand you, but this horse doesn't. If I lift my hands, he's gone . . . right over you." Then quickly, scornfully, Cherokee said, "Put that gun down! You might hurt an innocent horse." You'd have thought she was talking to a child.

Maybe it was the unexpected voice of a girl that did it, or maybe it was the raging attitude of Bullet Proof. Whatever it was, the gunman hesitated. There was a flickering moment of uncertainty on his part, something you could feel more than you could see. That's when I let Bullet Proof go . . . right at him.

He made another of those strange noises, kind of between a grunt and a curse, and jumped aside . . . but not in time. Bullet Proof caught him with his head and knocked him backwards almost under his own startled horse. Then both of us were off and on him. Cherokee had the gun and I had the man.

"Is he dead?" she asked. We sure seemed to be asking that question a lot.

"Just muddy," I said. "Keep the gun on him."

She seemed to like that. "Want me to put it against his throat?"

"If you like. Jam it in hard. They say it makes mean men real sweet and untalkative ones real talkative."

"That's what my daddy says," she said. "This one sure looks like a mean one."

38

He sure did. Smelled like one too. Had a jagged scar across his cheek, like maybe he had differed with an Apache at some time or another. Also had the biggest teeth I ever saw in a human's mouth. Looked like horse teeth. I shook him a little, and when he opened his eyes, I gave him time to feel the gun against his throat and then I said, "Talk."

He didn't seem to mind the gun. Probably used to havin' them stuck against his neck all the time. He twisted this way and that, payin' no attention to the gun barrel, and finally said, "Where's that . . . horse?" By the sound of his voice you could tell what he was scared of. Also he had that funny way of talkin', goin' "grunt" in between the words. At least it sounded like "grunt."

"Talk," I said.

"*Grunt*." He said it again, like a horse was standing on him. "Whatta ya wanta . . . *grunt* . . . know?" Just like a horse was standing on him.

"Everything," I said. "Start with why you're here and don't leave out a thing."

"I'm runnin' from the . . . *grunt* . . . law."

That was a pretty sorry start, even without the grunt. Everybody in Goodbye Gulch was runnin' from the law. It was the last refuge for every desperado in the southwest.

"Want me to cock the gun?" Cherokee asked me. I actually think she was enjoying it.

"That's a . . . *grunt* . . . hair trigger," he said.

Cherokee cocked it. She had to use both hands, and the gun barrel wobbled around under his chin a lot.

39

"Talk," I said.

He grunted. "Who are you?"

"Talk."

He grunted again. "You're in trouble."

"You're the one that's in trouble," Cherokee said.

He squirmed, a little nervous now, gruntin', "Watch that trigger. I tell you it's . . . *grunt* . . . hair."

"Talk."

He did. It all came out in a long series of grunts. Seemed kind of a fittin' way for a man like that to talk. The fact that we were holding him down in the mud made it seem even more fittin'. Maybe his smell added a little too.

"You messed us up," he grunted. "Spoilt things. Why'd you have to go and spoil things? We was gonna rob the bank at Bitter Wells, and maybe the Santa Fe train too. All we had to do was get the sheriff out of town. Everybody knows the . . . *grunt* . . . deppity is always . . . *grunt* . . . drunk."

That was the first time I had ever heard the grunt-deputy properly described. "Who's we?" I asked.

"Me and Dick Creel and some others."

"What's your name?"

He grunted to get started. "Folks calls me Grunt. Don't know why. My real name's Hector."

"Keep gruntin', Grunt," I said.

"Yes, 'cause if you don't," Cherokee said, "you will grunt your last." Comin' from her lips, it sounded like poetry.

Must have inspired me, 'cause I said, "And on your tombstone we will write *He Went Out Gruntin'*."

40

"Or," Cherokee said, "*Grunt Has Gone To His Reward*."

"Always . . . grunt . . . knew I'd come to a bad end. My . . . grunt . . . told me so."

"Grunt on, Grunt," I said.

He grunted on. "Dick Creel and the boys put out the word that old man Sheldon was dyin' and needed medicine. He figured the sheriff'd bring it up. Guess the sheriff's not as crazy as he thought."

"Sheriff's got hoof-and-mouth disease," I said. "Keep gruntin'."

"Dick Creel's mad because you messed us up. Says he's gonna make somebody pay. I was sent out to bring you in. I help around the jail and run errands for Dick Creel."

"Where do you live, Grunt?" I asked.

"In Outlaw," he grunted. "I sleep in the barn."

"Any pigs around?"

"A few," he grunted.

"I thought so."

"You sure did a terrible job of bringing us in, Grunt," Cherokee said.

"That's right," I said. "Don't you know better than to point a gun at an Osage horse?"

"Don't . . . grunt . . . mention that horse."

Behind us, his eye glintin' in the moonlight, Bullet Proof looked on, seeming endlessly intrigued by the mysterious gruntings of humans.

"Who's Dick Creel gonna make pay?" I asked.

"Said he figured you had folks and that folks will always pay to get their kin back. That's why he wants you alive. Says you're worth more alive than . . . *grunt* . . . dead."

"That makes sense," Cherokee said.

"How did Dick Creel know we were here?" I asked.

"Saw you cross the river just before the tornado. He even sent a rider to Bitter Wells to deliver the ransom note before the river rose."

"He sure works fast," Cherokee said.

"Sure does, ma'am," he grunted.

"If they pay the money, what happens?" I asked.

"We send a rider to get a second ransom. Dick Creel likes money. You're lucky he wants you alive."

"Where do we find Dick Creel?" I asked. I couldn't call him marshal. It would have debased the title.

"Him and eight of the boys live in Outlaw. In the . . . *grunt* . . . jail. They say it reminds 'em of the good old days when they was U.S. marshals."

"Nine U.S. marshals!"

"Countin' the . . . *grunt* . . . deppities."

Cherokee and I looked at each other in the moonlight across Grunt's foul and muddy body. It began to seem that we would go on through life like that, forever looking into each other's eyes across some desperado's body.

"Let him up," I said. His smell was beginning to bother me.

"Can I have my . . . *grunt* . . . gun back? It's a disgrace to lose your gun."

"Sure," I said. "Give me your holster."

When he had given me the holster, I told Cherokee to shake the bullets out of his gun. Then I put the gun in the holster and buckled the belt, hanging it around his neck.

"Now give me your other belt," I said.

"My pants'll fall off."

"Not when you're on your horse."

He unbuckled his belt and handed it to me, gruntin' all the while and looking occasionally at Bullet Proof.

"Turn around," I said. Then I knotted his hands up behind him with the belt and helped him get a foot in the stirrup. His pants did almost fall off before I finally got him in the saddle.

"Put the reins in his mouth," I told Cherokee, "and we'll head the horse for Kansas. If he opens his mouth the reins will fall out and the horse will stop. If he doesn't, well, maybe some kind sheriff up there will take them out for him." She hadn't yet got them in his mouth when I said, "I think we'll pay Dick Creel a visit in the morning."

"Tomorrow's Sunday," Grunt said. "The marshals always go to church on Sunday. Set in a special pew called Marshals Row. They're very religious."

"Do they wear their guns?"

"Sure. But it's against the rules to shoot in church." Just before Cherokee stuffed the reins in his mouth, he grunted again, "There's something else you oughta know."

"What's that?"

"Tom Beasley and his gang of outlaws want you too . . . dead. They think you're a tax collector. There's a bounty on tax collectors."

My head was beginning to swim with grunts and

43

ransoms and bounties and marshals and outlaws. It was almost like talking a different language, though I guessed if you lived in Goodbye Gulch for a while it would begin to seem natural.

"So," I said, "the marshals want us alive and the outlaws want us dead. Is that it?"

"Somethin' like that," he grunted. "Reverend Steel wants you too."

"For what?" Cherokee asked, still holding the reins.

"Prob'ly to save your soul," Grunt said. "He's real good at that. Dead shot, too."

It figured. "Look," I said. "If I'm a tax collector, what is she?" I nodded toward Cherokee, still holding the reins to stuff in his mouth.

"They say," he grunted, "that you're on your . . . *grunt* . . . honeymoon." Then he added, seeming to brag a little, "A tax collector was shot here onc't. In the church, I think."

"Who shot him?" Cherokee asked, quick.

He drew back, as if she had been about to strike him with the reins instead of stuff them in his mouth. "Can't tell you, ma'am. Took a . . . *grunt* . . . oath. Swore upon the altar. Gave my sacred . . . *grunt* . . . word."

I had had enough. "You can't ask a man to break his sacred grunt," I said to Cherokee. "Stuff the reins in his mouth."

She stuffed the reins in his mouth and he rode off in silence, except for the gruntin'.

7 ⋆ Uppers and Lowers

Goodbye Gulch was living up to its reputation for dishonoring all the sacred customs of civilized behavior. The only place I ever heard of where you could be wanted dead *and* alive. No wonder the marshal uttered that deathbed warning. Any place that wouldn't settle for you dead *or* alive was a place to keep away from. Everything about the gulch seemed to want to do you in. if the tornadoes didn't get you, the marshals would, and if the marshals didn't get you, the outlaws would; and if you survived all of that, you would probably end up gettin' done in by the preacher, Dead Shot Steel, or whatever his name was.

One thing about the place, it sure kept you on your toes. Reminded me of the marshal's advice about never sleeping unless you had to and then with one eye open. Also reminded me of those other words of his, "Know the kind of men you're up against." The Osages have a saying for it too—know your enemy—but Cherokee and I couldn't really call Dick Creel and Tom Beasley our enemies. They hadn't actually done anything yet to indicate they didn't like us. One of them just wanted us alive and the other wanted us dead, for reasons of their own, the reasons in both cases bein' money. I didn't figure it was anything personal. They would probably have shown the same regard for any passing stranger.

Sure made you suspicious though. Left you wondering what kind of men you were dealing with. You really didn't know where you stood.

When Grunt had disappeared down the trail, I said to Cherokee, "Wanta cut and run?"

She was trying to wipe Grunt's mud off her vest. "No. I came to get a confession and I'm going to get a confession. You wanta run?"

"No. And besides," I added, "we can't."

"Why not?"

"The river's up. Only a desperado or someone runnin' from the law would try to cross it."

Wiping at the mud, she smiled in the moonlight. "Looks like we stay, then, doesn't it?"

I liked the way she said it. And I liked the way she smiled. I even liked the way she wiped her muddy hands on her horse's tail. "Looks like it," I said. "Did you bring any food?"

"A little hardtack and some dried beef and a canteen of water. It'll keep us alive. How about you?"

"Just hymnbooks and whisky," I said. Somehow, there in Goodbye Gulch before dawn on a Sunday morning, they seemed to go together. Nourishment for sinning and nourishment for repentance. They fit the place, like shooting tax collectors in the church. "Also," I said, "I've got a spade, if it comes to that, and a shroud." It sounded like music. "The Hymn of the West," or something like that. Hymnbooks and whisky, spades and shrouds, the very soul of the Territory lashed to my saddle.

"Do you really drink?" she asked.

Somehow I wished I did. I wished I was a little taller too. And I wished I had a reputation for being hard as nails. But most of all I wished my long, black, non-existent mustache drooped.

"It was for old man Sheldon," I said.

"That's what I figured."

I was glad she didn't say anything about it being sinful. You couldn't have "The Hymn of the West" without whisky any more than you could have "The Hymn of the West" without hymnbooks and spades and Osage horses.

Which reminded me. "Can you twitch a horse?"

"Sure," she said.

"I want him on your side," I said, meaning Bullet Proof.

And I think it was there I saw that "The Hymn of the West" had beauties that I would never understand, at least regarding women and horses. For it wasn't necessary that she gain his loyalty. She just went over to him and ran her hand along his head. The wild glint in his eye softened as he tossed his nose high once and brought it down against her cheek with what seemed like a tender slobber of devotion.

"Let's ride," I said, before the tenderness got out of hand. That horse actually had a kind of lovelight in his eye. You couldn't much blame him. Even with Grunt's mud on her she was as pretty as a colt.

"Where we headin'?" she asked, climbing on her horse.

"For the jail in Outlaw. I wanta know the kind of men we're up against."

"One thing is certain," she said. "They're crazy."

It didn't take us long to find Outlaw. Bullet Proof sniffed it out in no time. It lay at the bottom of a hill about halfway between old man Sheldon's mine and the river. We had almost run right through it gettin' away from the tornado, which was how, I guessed, Dick Creel had seen us.

There wasn't much to the place. Other than a jail and a church and a saloon and a livery barn—all of them old—it had only a few ramshackle houses scattered around in the plum thickets. Looked just like what it was, a refuge for outlaws.

Our luck was running good. In the window of the jail a kerosene lamp was burning, the wick turned low.

"For wayfaring outlaws," I explained. "It lights their way to home."

We rode slowly down the slope and into the town. There was still about an hour of darkness left. No one was stirring.

"If a dog barks, run," I said.

"Don't worry," she whispered.

But no dog barked. We rode quietly up to the window of the jail and looked in.

It was a sight to see. I couldn't keep from getting off Bullet Proof to get a better look. Cherokee followed, and for a moment we stood with our noses to the window, not quite believing.

Nine cots, one of them empty—for the Bitter Wells ransom rider, I supposed—stood neatly in a row in the outer office of the jail. Cot by cot, side by side, flat upon their backs slept eight ex-U.S. marshals. Cot by cot, side by side, their boots stood at the ready. Cot by cot, side by side, their holsters hung pegged on the cots. Cot by cot, side by side, their hats lay on the floor beneath the guns. Cot by cot, side by side, their socks were on their feet, the feet all pointing upward in a row. Cot by cot, side by side, their marshals' badges gleamed upon their tunics. And just behind each cot, side by side, on eight little tables stood eight pairs of false teeth and as many pairs of spectacles. Oh, it was a sight to see. The teeth were grinning at us. The spectacles were staring. And to myself I thought, "Toothless renegades. That's the kind of men they are. The world has passed them by. No more territories. No more official orders. No more anything."

"Look over there," Cherokee whispered, pointing to the cells.

I pressed my nose against the glass. Behind us our horses stood, their noses forward, curious as we were. There on the floor of the cell in dirty disorder five shabby outlaws lay sleeping behind the bars, where, I fancied, they slept best. Some leaned against the wall, their hats down over their eyes. Others sprawled on the wooden floor. All slept with their boots on and their guns in their hands, and all were as old or older than the marshals. The world had passed them by too.

"Tom Beasley and his boys," I whispered.

"The ones that want us dead. The bounty hunters."

They looked half dead themselves. The marshals looked completely dead, laid out as they were so neatly in military style. You could even read the inscription stamped on each item of their trade. U.S. Government cots. U.S. Government blankets. U.S. Government guns. U.S. Government holsters. U.S. Government boots. U.S. Government socks. And I knew that somewhere in tiny letters not visible to us there was stamped upon the rims of the glasses, U.S. Government spectacles, and upon the edges of the gums, U.S. Government teeth. It simply could have been no other way.

I think that was where an idea came to me. "Maybe I could get them," I said.

"The boots?"

"No. The glasses, and maybe the teeth too. That would just about reduce them to a state of total surrender."

"Why not just take their guns?"

"They probably got a whole arsenal somewhere."

"That still leaves the outlaws. And they're the ones that want us dead. Do you suppose we could get their guns?"

"'Fraid not. The cell is locked. The marshals probably lock the outlaws in every night so both sides will feel comfortable."

"They're playin' a game," she said.

"Yes, but the bullets are real."

And though the bullets were real, I knew it was the only thing that remained of their vanished glory. The rest was ritual. I could see them—marshals and outlaws—going through the motions, changing the guard, so to speak, each evening after sunset. Without the ritual, neither side would have slept in peace—the culprits in the cells, the fierce lawmen on the cots, according to the rules.

The grinning teeth and staring spectacles grinned and stared at us . . . invitingly, I thought. They seemed to be begging to be taken, especially the teeth, smiling so broadly and unceasingly. In the crazy game we were playing, Cherokee and I didn't have any advantages. The teeth seemed to be saying, "We will make the difference. Take us with you."

"Hold the horses," I said, "and be ready to run. I may have to come out fast."

Then I slipped in through the door.

From the back cell I could hear the rise and fall of snoring. The outlaws—securely locked in—were peaceful and content. So, it seemed, were the marshals, making very little noise as they slept, as if to do so were against some written order in the U.S. Marshal's Manual. Now and then there was a small snort, but nothing stretched out, no whistling or blubbering. My main trouble was in getting behind the cots. They stretched from wall to wall and were only a foot apart, which I figured was probably regulation too. There was no way but to step between them and over the boots and hats and by the guns. That's what I did. It was dangerous stepping. I had forgotten to take my spurs off. Also I hadn't figured on the noise that eight pairs of false teeth and spectacles make when you carry them heaped in your cupped hands. They rattle unmercifully. The uppers seemed to be tryin' to chatter with the lowers. Trying to keep them quiet, I started making my way back over the hats and boots between the beds and to the door. That was when I heard somebody roll over and a voice I figured was Dick Creel's say, "That you, Gerhart?"

I stopped, dead still.

Again the voice. "That you, Tinklehoff?"

I didn't breathe.

Again the voice. "That you, Mitgang?"

I took off, leaping the boots and bolting through the door. Not a second too soon either. From inside I could hear the crash of tables falling as the marshals reached for their teeth and spectacles and boots and guns. Holding the loot in one hand, I made a jump into the stirrup and Bullet Proof was off. Behind us I heard Dick Creel shouting, "It's the damn Comanches! After 'em!" Then I heard the sound of gunfire in the air. Sounded like it went right straight up through the roof.

8 * Hangmen's Knots and Tree Limbs

We ran hard for about five miles, skirting the hills back of Dead Horse Crossing and keeping out of sight. Daylight had come now, and when we finally pulled up behind a clump of sumac bushes, we could see the Nescatunga River in the distance. It was running full, carrying with it a lot of silt and trees and other debris ripped up by the tornado. I knew it would be another day or two before anybody could safely cross it.

I put the false teeth and spectacles in my saddlebags with the whisky, taking care not to smash anything. Didn't want any loose teeth rattling around, or loose lenses either. Had enough things to keep track of as it was—shovels and shrouds and hymnbooks, not to mention the matches and the herbs.

That was our first real victory in Goodbye Gulch, if you didn't count the tornado we had outrun and the reviving of old man Sheldon. I didn't figure Grunt counted. Cherokee and I both felt better. There's nothing like a well-executed raid, even if it's on false teeth and spectacles, to send a little feeling of excitement through you. Kind of makes you feel like you're in command. Trouble was, we didn't have time to enjoy it. I had just got my spoils settled in the saddlebag when Bullet Proof flung up his head and snorted.

"He smells trouble," Cherokee said.

"Yes. But where?"

He snorted again.

"I think it's the river," she said.

"I think you're right."

And then I saw it, but I didn't quite believe it. A man, hanging to the tail of a struggling horse, was midstream in the current of the Nescatunga. Only the horse's head was visible, and in back the man's bobbing hat. That was no place for a man or horse to be, and it was clear, even from where we were, that the horse was already in trouble.

"They're not gonna make it," Cherokee said. "Wonder who he is?"

"Runnin' from the law," I said. "Who else would try to swim a horse across that river?"

"Even so . . ." she said, but didn't finish.

Even so I knew what she meant. Runnin' from the law or not, he had to be helped. We had to do it. At least we had to try. We couldn't sit there and watch a human drown, not even in Goodbye Gulch, where gratitude more likely than not meant a gun pointed at you.

Neither of us said anything else. We didn't have to. We knew—even our horses knew—that you always save a man's life first and then deal with him later, if you have to. We also knew that you might get shot for your troubles, but that didn't mean you didn't try. That—like so many other things—went with the Territory. And so we rode, uncautious, down the hill, judging as we went the spot where the current would most likely sweep them to the shore. The horse was still about thirty yards out in the stream and struggling wildly when we got there. His upflung head, magnificent in the morning sun, seemed to be defying all the unknown treacheries of that watery world.

Very softly Cherokee said, "Think he'll make it?"

"If wantin' to means anything, he will."

Very softly, like a prayer, she said, "Come on, horse."

We were off then and at the river's edge, each with a lariat. Then I saw something. "What do you think of that?"

"He's got a gun in his hand," she said.

"It figures."

He was holding the gun in one hand and the horse's tail with the other. I should have known. Any man fording a flooding river into Goodbye Gulch would come no other way.

"Maybe he's been shot," Cherokee said. "Head's hangin' down a little."

"He's still alive," I said, "though he must be full of water."

"We can't help that horse," she said, her words carrying a tone of helpless urging.

"That's right. He's got to do it on his own. He didn't choose to cross that river—too wise for that—but now he's got to do it."

"Come on, horse," she said again, still as soft as a prayer.

The current was pulling the struggling, flailing horse in a little closer. You could see his eyes now, wild with wonder and disbelief at finding something stronger than he was. He was a good horse, a magnificent horse, but most of all a horse that wanted to reach that river bank. Behind him the man's head sagged in the water, the hand with the pistol still high in the air.

"I'm gonna lasso him," I said.

"The horse?"

"No. He needs all the air he can get."

"He sure does. He needs it bad. Come on, horse!" She was shoutin' now.

I swung the lariat, the loop settling down around the man's head on the first try.

"You got him!" she said.

"By the neck!"

"Pull," she shouted. "It'll take the weight off the horse."

I dug my heels into the grass and pulled, hard enough it seemed to pull his head off. And still he held the gun and still he held the tail. But my pulling eased the horse's load. He sensed it and in one last violent burst of energy came lunging and crashing wild-eyed up the bank, standing on legs that trembled and wobbled like those of a new-born colt. He had barely enough strength left to keep from falling. Behind him the man with the lariat around his neck was still gripping the tail with one hand and the gun with the other.

We had to pry them both loose.

"I'll bet his finger's on the trigger," Cherokee said.

"Probably is. Stay out of the line of fire."

He was a big old guy and a soggy mess. Looked like a giant hog that had just been dipped in a vat. Water was running from his hat and flowing freely from holes in the soles of his boots. But that gun was dry. When we finally got it out of his hand, I gave it to Cherokee and then I straddled him and started pushin'.

"What are you doin'?" she asked.

"Got to pump the water out of him."

"Can I help?"

"Yes. Dig a little sewer under his mouth so the water will run off."

She was down on her knees in the mud beside him then, and I was straddlin' him . . . or tryin' to. He was as big as a bull.

"There's lots of water comin' out," she said, peering up under his head. "Mostly through his nose."

There sure was. He must have swallowed a tubful. I couldn't keep from wondering how much water a big man like that could hold. For sure it had to be measured in tubs or barrels.

"Is he breathing?" I asked, wondering how many times I had heard those words in the last few hours.

"Just gurgling," she said. "Keep pumping."

"It might help to loosen the rope around his neck."

"I hadn't thought about that."

She loosened the lariat, and I heard a kind of blubbering whoosh all at once up front somewhere and saw Cherokee wiping her face.

"That did it," she said.

"How's his breathing?"

"Can't hear it for the gurgling."

I stopped pumping for a moment and listened. Cherokee and I looked at each other across the water-logged body. It seemed we never would quit looking at each other across shotguns, pistols, or dying men.

"He's breathing," I said. "Let's turn him over. Not all the way. Just enough to get a look at him and still let the water run out."

"His tongue looks a little blue," she said, down on her knees trying to pry his mouth open.

"Give me a hand," I said.

It wasn't easy but we finally got him partly turned over. He was breathing pretty well by then, gurgling good. With the sound of water running from the soles of his boots, he sounded like a leaky tub. Kind of looked like one too. Sure was a fat fellow. No wonder that horse had almost gone under. Must have weighed three hundred pounds. I couldn't keep from wondering what he would have weighed dressed, as they say. Though he had holes in his boots and holes in his hat, I couldn't find any holes in him. Didn't seem to be wounded. Except for his tongue, which, as Cherokee said, was blue and lolling a little, and his eyes, which looked a little glassy, he seemed all right. I was holding him up as best I could and Cherokee was flat on her stomach in the mud trying to inspect him. Finally she looked up and said, "He's wearin' a badge. Says U.S. Marshal. Think he's a real one?"

"Not a chance," I said.

"How can you tell?"

"By the smell. Real marshals bathe every two weeks—regulations." I didn't tell her I had read that in a book by what was beginning to look like the only true and honest marshal the West had ever known—Geoffrey Tolliver.

"It'd take a pretty big tub for this one," she said.

"It'd take a horse tank."

"Wait!" she said. Her nose was almost buried in the sewer she had dug. She was trying to get at something. Behind us the horses stood, snortin' quietly, their noses out in our direction, seeming curious and intrigued by this latest kind of attention that humans give to humans. You couldn't much blame them. If I had been a horse I'd have been puzzled too. "It's a letter," she said, "in his vest pocket. I got it!"

That was when the horses jumped, but not at us, at something farther off.

"Riders," I said. "In the distance."

And that was where the man blinked once and looked up at us out of the corner of his eye. It wasn't glassy now. You could see he was gonna live a while, if some kind soul didn't shoot him for mistreatin' horses. I shook him a little to see if his tongue still flopped, and then I said, "What's your name?"

"Fats," he blubbered. "Folks calls me Fats."

"That figures."

"Where's ol' Dick?" he blubbered, his head lyin' in the sewer. And then he made a blubbery moan, sayin', "I think I'm goin' out. It's the end of the trail. Crossed my last river. Got to make my last request. Give ol' Dick my dyin' words."

He was convinced he was dyin', and wallowin' in the pleasure of his convictions. I knew the mentality, and I also knew the language. So I said, "Sure, stranger, what do you want us to carve on your slab?"

Even in the mud the words sounded like music.

"Give ol' Dick the letter in my pocket," he blubbered, "so he'll know ol' Fats carried out his orders." Choking sadly, he let a little water leak from his mouth and said, "Tell him I died in the saddle." He made it sound glorious, sad, and pitiful. Then he let his head flop again and his tongue fall out, figuring, I guessed, that since he had spoken the proper words he would just naturally die. But he went on breathing and gurgling easy, his nose resting in the grass. It was a good performance.

"You want us to send a letter to your mother?" I asked.

He moaned a little, which I figured meant yes.

"Hurry!" Cherokee said. "They're gettin' closer."

I hurried, reluctantly, wishing Fats would gurgle out more dyin' phrases. It wasn't every day you got to hear them from the lips of a man who really believed them.

"Hurry!" Cherokee shouted again.

I leaped on Bullet Proof. He was running before my right leg hit the other side of the saddle.

"They're shootin'!" Cherokee said, as we ran. "Must be the ones that want us dead."

A bullet whistled over my head. "I figure you're right," I shouted in the wind. But I wasn't too sure. It might have been those dim-eyed old marshals shootin' at us without their glasses on. If they wanted us alive and were shootin' to miss us, that more likely than not meant that they would hit us, since old men never hit what they shoot at anyway, with or without their glasses.

I led the way, or rather Bullet Proof led the way. And I was thinking, "Leave it to an Osage to name a horse Bullet Proof. If it works, it's fine. But if it doesn't, the joke's a bad one."

It worked. At least that time. We pulled away from

them without gettin' hit and headed for the western hills. It wasn't until we were high and safe at the edge of the first rimrocks that I pulled up. Whoever they were —the ones that wanted us dead or the ones that wanted us alive—they had turned back, probably to listen to Fats gurgle out a few more last requests and dyin' words, or more probably because they wanted that ransom message worse than they wanted us right then. Old Fats was gonna be in trouble if he didn't produce the ransom note. The marshals would probably court-martial him or something. But I figured he could always blame his bad fortune on the "damn Comanches," the way the marshals did when we stole their teeth. The crazy part was, the marshals would probably believe him.

"You got the letter?" I asked Cherokee.

"Sure."

And then I realized something. "Cherokee," I said, "we made a terrible mistake."

"You mean we should have shot it out?" She was still holding Fats's gun.

"No. I mean we really shouldn't have left that rope around his neck. Looks bad. Particularly with that tree limb right above him."

"Sure does," she said. And then she brightened up again. "But it didn't have a hangman's knot in it. They're old lawmen. They'll understand."

Trigger fingers and hangmen's knots. Tree limbs and lariats. Crazy marshals and Comanches. I didn't know— because I wasn't there—but that must have been the way it sounded when you said it in the old days.

"What does it say?" I asked.

She was already reading the letter.

9 ★ Amazing Grace

Or trying to. "The ink's all wet and blotty," she said. "It's hard to make out. Smells a little too."

"Guess old Fats had it pretty close to his body. Hold it in the sun till it dries, and wave it in the air until the smell disappears."

That's what she did. Then we got off our horses and sat down on a rock and tried to figure it out. It took a while, but finally we did it, somewhat to my regret I've got to say.

Bitter Wells
Oklahoma Territory
1907

Marshal Creel
Outlaw Territory
Dear Marshal Creel:
The Mayor of Bitter Wells is pleased to inform you that the boy being held in your territorial jurisdiction for wanton acts of destruction, endangerment of lives and property, and other high crimes and misdemeanors, is probably one Territory Gore, son of Marie Louise and Lafayette Gore (both deceased).

The Mayor is further pleased to inform you that Bitter Wells can not pay nine hundred ($900) dollars for safe return of same in good condition or five hundred ($500) dollars for unsafe return of same in poor condition, as you suggest in your very kind letter. First, it is Saturday night and everyone is drunk and tomorrow is Sunday and the bank is closed. Also the price is too high for a kid, though he does have with him a very good horse we would like back.

We do not know the girl you speak of. She is probably running from the law.

With firm, official regards,
S. Bicker, Mayor

"That's real nice," Cherokee said. "One bunch wants us alive, another bunch wants us dead, and that last bunch doesn't want us either way."

"Those marshals sure didn't put much of a price on us." I was a little hurt.

She patted my muddy arm with her muddy hand. "Don't feel bad, Territory. There's a lot of injustice in the world."

Actually it wasn't the injustice that bothered me as much as it was the general insanity. Seemed to be catching. Now my fellow citizens were acting as crazy as the marshals. I could even begin to feel it rubbing off on me.

"Cherokee, have you still got your fountain pen and a sheet of paper?"

"Only paper I've got is the confession. What you got in mind?"

"Think I'll let Dick Creel get his letter."

"This letter?"

"No. The one we're gonna write."

Her face brightened. She saw the beauty of it too. "It'll work!" she said.

"At least it'll give us some time, maybe enough for the river to go down, in case we have to make a run for it."

"You don't suppose Fats read the letter, do you?"

"Fats can't read," I said. "He's not the kind."

"We can't write it on the confession. That's my only copy."

"We'll use a page from the hymnbook."

I got the hymnbook from my saddlebag and tore out the back page. There was nothing on it except some faint lettering which said Property of Methodist Church. That seemed to give our efforts a special blessing.

"Make it good," she said.

"I'll do my best."

With her leaning over my shoulder and the horses regarding us with what seemed concern and sympathy, I scratched out the letter.

> Bitter Wells
> Oklahoma Territory
> 1907
>
> Marshal Creel
> Outlaw Territory
> Dear Marshal Creel:
> The Mayor of Bitter Wells is pleased to inform you that the persons you are holding in your territorial jurisdiction for wanton destruction of property, endangerment of lives, and other high crimes and misdemeanors, are highly honored, deeply loved, and greatly respected citizens. One is the Territorial Governor's son and the other is

General Duncan's daughter. We will gladly pay the price you request for their return, provided, of course, that you keep them safe from harm and in good condition. The money will be delivered within a few days by special messenger. Please give him safe passage. Meanwhile, if you allow no one to harm a hair of their beloved heads, we may be able to reward you further for your kindnesses and put in a good word for you with the Governor and the General.

Affectionate, official regards,
S. Bicker, Mayor

"It's beautiful," Cherokee said. Her eyes were shining with admiration. "Now the marshals will have to protect us from the outlaws. Maybe we shouldn't have taken their teeth and their glasses."

"We didn't know that then. Doesn't matter anyway. They probably shoot about as straight without glasses as they do with them."

"One thing is certain. They'll raise the price on our heads for sure now."

"That's right," I said. "And while they're doing it, they'll be very careful not to touch a single hair of our beloved heads."

"When do we deliver the letter?"

"Tonight at prayer meeting time. I imagine those old renegades pray awfully long and hard."

"Do you suppose that when they bow their heads they dream they're in heaven chasing wrongdoers?"

"Cherokee," I said, "I think you are a little touched in your beloved head."

"I know," she said. "It runs in the family. They call

my daddy Crazy Ed. But then, so are you. That's why we will win."

It was nice to know. And there went old Santoo.

She was nice to know too, gettin' nicer all the time. Daughter of Crazy Ed and a Cherokee mother named Moonon-Moonon, or something on that order. Mud from head to toe and dead from lack of sleep, but nice to know. She went with the rimrocks and the wild plum bushes, with the Nescatunga, even with the hangmen's knots and tree limbs. *Cherokee Waters . . . Cherokee Waters . . . youngest and fairest of Moonon's daughters.* You didn't even need a guitar.

I folded the letter, wrote the marshal's name on the outside, and put it in the hymnbook between "There's a Blue Sky a-Way up Yonder" and "Showers of Blessing," both of which seemed filled with promises that we could certainly use, no matter what the weather.

It was getting along toward noon now and we didn't have much time to waste if we were going to get back to Outlaw in time to scout the place before dark. Also I didn't want Cherokee to start thinking about food or sleep, both of them very sweet to think about right then. I knew that if we ate, sleep would follow. It was a chance we couldn't afford to take. She knew it too, and just like me, she didn't mention hardtack or dried beef. Instead, we drank a little water from the canteen, and then I said, "Reckon we better move out. It's a long ride and we have to keep to the hills. There's no telling what the marshals are up to."

"One thing's for sure," she said. "They're up to something."

And she was right. We hadn't ridden more than five miles, working our way slowly along the canyons and gullies, when we came across some big posters nailed to the trees. Scrawled hastily in black pencil and in lines that looked like they had been done by someone with poor eyesight, they read:

WANTED (ALIVE)
FOR THE ATTEMPTED HANGIN' OF DPTY
U.S. MARSHAL FATS TUBSTYLE—TWO
ARMED AND VICIOUS CRIMINALS. ONE
ON BLUE GRAY GELDING. OTHER ON
CHESTNUT WITH STOCKING FEET. REWARD
FOR INFORMATION LEADING TO CAPTURE.
MARSHAL DICK CREEL

"They're sure ungrateful," Cherokee said. "After all the water we pumped out of Fats."

"They're probably still pumping on him."

But I knew that if they were doing any pumping on Fats it was to pump the letter out of him. Until they got that, they didn't know anything for sure in the game they were playing, except that they would all be eating soup for a while and loading their guns by feel.

We kept to the canyons and gullies, slow and cautious. The sun was just beginning to disappear when we finally slipped along a canyon to the hills above Outlaw. Sleep had gone by that time, and hunger too, their places taken by excitement. Keeping to the cover of the rocks, we got off our horses and crawled the last few feet to the top.

"Looks awful quiet," Cherokee said.

"That's Sunday evening quietness. Being wrongdoers and lawbreakers, they're all very religious. Wrongdoers and lawbreakers only put their faith in two things," I explained, not telling her where I had got my information. "The good Lord and a Colt forty-five. If one fails 'em, they've always got the other to fall back on. Usually, though, they don't do too much shootin' on Sunday."

"They shot at us."

"They'll probably repent at the services tonight, especially if the sermon is good."

"I won't forgive 'em."

"They won't be askin' you. Look! They're beginning to gather."

There was just enough light to make out the figures as they moved along the streets. The church bell was ringing, and at the door of the church a group of men dressed in black stood side by side to greet the faithful.

"Must be the deacons," Cherokee said.

"That's right. All of them ex-U.S. marshals. Deacon-marshals, I guess you'd call them."

The church door closed then behind the deacon-marshals, and just faintly you could hear the voices rising.

"They sing good," Cherokee said.

"That's because they mean it. Come on . . . let's deliver the letter. When they find it, they'll think it's a message from heaven, especially when they read the part about the money."

We got on our horses and rode slowly through the brush down the hill, to the rising strains of

Amazing Grace, how sweet the sound,
That saved a wretch like me

Never from the voices of humans had I heard such fittin' words. It was, I think, the "wretch" that did it. If the good Lord was not moved, he was unmovable. Out of the mouths of wretches, I was thinking, knowing it was out of the mouths of something else, but going on thinking anyway. Out of the mouths of wretches comes the beauty of desperation.

> *I once was lost, but now am found,*
> *Once was blind, but now I see*

Utterly desperate. Utterly beautiful.

"Don't they do it good?" Cherokee marveled. We had stopped our horses to listen.

"Like angels," I said. And it was true. If you hadn't known better, you might have thought you were in Heaven. Even the stars around us seemed to suggest that we had been shot and killed earlier that day and were now riding down a slope in Paradise.

When they had finished, we rode on. By the time we reached the back of the jail, the congregation was soaring in song again, now singing "Keep My Soul From Harm and Hurt." Since the jail was right next to the church, and the windows were open, we had to make our movements under cover of song and sermon. Out into the night came the voices of the faithful as they sang:

> *O cleanse the vile*
> *Unseemly dirt,*
> *O keep my soul*
> *From harm and hurt*

Desperadoes of the soul, they were. It was that "harm and hurt" that touched you, and their wish to cleanse the "vile unseemly dirt."

"Powerful pretty," Cherokee said. "They sing like true believers."

"It's all they got left."

"Thought you said they had their guns."

"They do, for a little while yet. But they know that's runnin' out on them. They're almost at the end of their rope."

"Listen!" she said, marveling.

> *My leaden heart*
> *Once bulletproof,*
> *Now soars on high*
> *To heaven's roof*

Marshals, renegades, outlaws. In the church they hoped to cleanse the vile unseemly dirt and soften the lead in their bulletproof hearts. Tomorrow they would return to their usual ways, or maybe before the night was over, but for a little while they'd ask the Lord to save their soul from harm and hurt. And were it saved from harm and hurt, it would for certain be Amazing Grace—which they perhaps knew better than anyone else.

They were on the last verse when Cherokee and I hid our horses behind the old livery barn and slipped up to the back door of the jail. I had the letter in my hand.

> *O cleanse the vile*
> *Unseemly dirt,*

O keep my soul
From harm and hurt

The music stopped then, and the night was suddenly quiet. But only for a moment. The preacher had risen. We could see him through the open window. That, I guessed, would be Dead Shot Steel. Nodding toward the deacons in Marshals Row and to what maybe were the aldermen in Outlaws Row, he said, "Brother Richard Creel, would you please intone the Marshal's Creed?"

Dick Creel stood tall and straight, armed and toothless, while starting to recite the Marshal's Creed.

"Now we can go," I whispered.

"Wait!" She grabbed my arm. "I want to hear it."

"I'll teach it to you later."

"You mean you know it?"

"Sure. It's called The Holy Creed and Prayer of a U.S. Marshal. It just says that you're always supposed to be lookin' for wanted men and that if there aren't any around you're supposed to go out and dig up a few because in an unlaw-abiding world like ours there is always somebody that is wanted for something. And then you ask the Lord to help you hunt him down. Let's go."

But Dick Creel was finished, and Dead Shot Steel had come back to the pulpit. I noticed he was wearing two guns, like the deacon-marshals and the aldermen-outlaws. "Brother Tom Beasley," said the preacher, "would you please intone the Outlaw's Code?"

"Now we can go," Cherokee said.

"Wait!" I grabbed her arm. "I want to hear it."

"I'll tell it to you later."

"You mean you know it?"

"Sure. It's called The Holy Code and Prayer of A Wanted Man. My daddy taught it to me when I was little. It just says you're supposed to be runnin' from the law all your life because you're a wanted man and even if you're innocent it doesn't matter because if you're runnin', a U.S. marshal will start chasing you and hound you to the end of your days. And then you ask the Lord to help you bushwack him. Let's go."

"Wait a minute." Alderman-outlaw Tom had sat down, shiftin' up his guns a little, and Dead Shot Steel had stood back up, shiftin' his a little and saying, "Brother El Hidalgo del Pecos Rio, would you please make a translation of the Creed and the Code for the benefit of our Spanish-speaking faithful on the run?"

Brother El Hidalgo stopped strapping his knife on his boot, rose and fondled the brim of his sombrero, which he kept pulled down tight across his eyes, and then spoke the Creed and the Code, with particular devotion to the latter. When he sat down, Preacher Dead Shot Steel said, "My sermon for tonight is Love." Hitching up his guns, he began.

"Now's the time," we both said at once.

We eased the door open and stepped inside. The kerosene lamp, standing as a beacon for wayfaring outlaws, was turned down low. The jail was quiet.

"It smells," Cherokee said.

"Nine marshals gone bad live here," I explained. "And about a half-dozen old outlaws."

"That looks like Dick Creel's desk over there by the lamp," she said. "It's got a shotgun behind it."

"Turn up the lamp."

She turned the lamp up a little. The old shotgun looked like it hadn't been used for thirty years. The stock was almost falling off. I put the letter down on the desk beside the lamp, and just as I was turning to inspect what looked like the oldest jail in the West, Cherokee said, "Territory! Somebody's coming!"

We just had time to duck behind another desk in the corner. Then Dick Creel walked in through the back door, followed by two other deacons or marshals or whatever they were. Whatever they were, they looked murderous, especially for men who had just come from church.

"Sombody turned that lamp up!" Dick Creel shouted. "Saw it out of the corner of my eye."

We crouched, waitin'—my spurs diggin' without mercy into my backside.

10 ★ A Three Way Split

"Somethin's amiss here!" Dick Creel roared, standing in the middle of the jail.

"Why'd you draw your guns, Chief?" one of the deacon-marshals asked.

"Because you never know . . . you never know," Dick Creel said mysteriously, popping his guns back in the direction of their holsters. One of the guns missed and clattered to the floor. Creel bent over and felt around until he found it, then picked it up, spun the chamber a time or two and said, "Somebody turned that lamp up, Gerhart. I saw it while the preacher was a-preachin'."

"That's why you're known as the man who sees everything," Gerhart said.

"And the man who's never caught off guard," said the other deacon-marshal.

"And don't you forget it!" roared Dick Creel, squintin' in all directions and poppin' his guns.

"Don't know how we got out of church in the middle of the sermon," Gerhart said, "without old Dead Shot drawin' his guns on us."

"He had his eyes closed," Dick Creel said, "a-butterin'

up the Lord. And besides, if he had drawn, I'd have shot back."

"That's why you're known as the man who never argues," Gerhart said.

"And don't you forget it!" Dick Creel roared. "Got to keep order in my territory. You can't sleep, you can't argue, and if you shoot, you better not miss."

"Amen," the others said. Sounded like they were still in church.

"Well, now, what's this?" Dick Creel shouted, seeing the letter by the lamp. "Somebody left a note."

"Why'd you draw your gun, Marshal?" Gerhart asked.

"Because you never know . . . you never know," Dick Creel said. "It might be a Comanche trick. Damn Comanches'll do anything. Steal you blind and bleed you white." He stomped over and reached for the letter.

That's where a little trouble developed. Dick Creel's vision caused him to bump the letter with his hand, knocking it over to the edge of the desk. It teetered there but didn't fall. If it had fallen to the floor, we would have been dead. We were only a couple of feet away and he still had that gun in his hand. I was crouching way down now, my spurs chewing into my hind parts. I think I was actually drawing blood. Dick Creel reached for the letter again. And I just knew he was going to knock it off this time. That really would have been the end. We were almost right underneath the teetering letter. I forgot all about my spurs and the damage they were doing and reached out and put my finger tip against the letter to keep it from going over the edge. Sure enough, he misjudged again, hittin' it with a bony finger hard enough to knock a hole in the desk. It slid a little. I kept holdin' it up, my side higher than the side on the desk. If he hadn't been nine-tenths blind, he would have seen that it was practically standing on end. I even thought about handing it to him. But then he got it, yanking it up hard, and I went back to resting on my rowels.

"Where's my glasses, Gerhart?" he shouted.

"The raiders stole 'em," Gerhart said.

"Damn Comanches!" Creel muttered. "I'll round 'em all up someday and bring 'em in." He thrust the letter out to Gerhart. "Here. You read it."

"They stole my glasses too," Gerhart said.

"That's no excuse," Creel said. "An order is an order." Then he turned to the other deacon-marshal and gave another order. "Bring me the magnifying glass, Tinklehoff. Step lively!" Tinklehoff found the magnifying glass on the desk right over our heads. "There, that's better," Dick Creel said, holding the magnifying glass and the gun in the same hand as he leaned over the letter. "Looks official," he said. "Says Property of Methodist Church. Wait a minute. There's something else here." He peered and twisted and squinted, the gun twisting around his head with him, then he rose up to his full six feet four and said, "Total victory, men. Total victory. We've got the Governor's son and the General's daughter. We won!"

"That's why you're known as the man who never loses," Tinklehoff said.

"And don't you forget it!" Dick Creel said. "When I run a territory, I run a territory."

"That's why you're known as the man who . . ." But Gerhart didn't finish, because the door swung open and in walked Tom Beasley flanked by two outlaws. Through the open window you could hear Dead Shot Steel still sermonizing on the subject of Love.

"Who's there!" Dick Creel roared at the outlaws. He was lookin' right at Tom Beasley.

"Why you holdin' the gun?" Tom Beasley asked.

"Because you never know . . . you never know," Dick Creel said. "Why aren't you in church, like all God-fearing men?"

"Why aren't you?" Tom Beasley asked. "It's because you're up to somethin', that's why."

"That's why you're known as the man who's always up to somethin'," one of the outlaws said.

"What are you holdin' in your hand?" Beasley asked. "Besides the gun, I mean."

"It's official," Dick Creel said. "Confidential."

Tom Beasley snatched the letter. "Read it, Hidalgo."

"I don't read English," Hidalgo said.

Tom Beasley snatched the letter back and shoved it at the other outlaw. "Read it, Pawnee."

"I don't read English neither," Pawnee said.

Tom Beasley muttered something about "ignorant outlaws" and then took the letter himself, pretending to read. He held it a long time, turning it around various ways, then finally he said, "Tell you what. We'll split two ways."

"Fair enough," Dick Creel said.

I had a feelin' Tom Beasley won that hand on a bluff.

"Let's shake on it," Beasley said.

"Yeah," said Hidalgo.

"Yeah," said Pawnee.

While they were shaking, the door swung open and Dead Shot Steel the preacher walked in, his gun in his hand. Behind him the voices were rising high in song again.

> O grant me still
> The needful days
> To ease my soul
> And mend my ways

"Why aren't you deacons and aldermen in church where God-fearin' men are supposed to be?" asked Dead Shot Steel.

"Official business," Dick Creel snapped. "Special delivery letter."

"Yeah," Tom Beasley said.

Dead Shot Steel snatched the letter from Tom Beasley's hand and read it. "That's a shameful business," he said. "Plottin' behind my back. What's this town comin' to? We'll split three ways."

"Fair enough," said Dick Creel.

"Fair enough," said Tom Beasley.

"Lift your right hand," Dick Creel said, "and swear after me."

He had his gun in his right hand. In fact, all of them had their guns in their right hands. They lifted them and swore after Dick Creel that they would catch the two marauders in the gulch before sundown of another day, so help them God. "From now on," said Creel, "they're runnin' from the law, and the law is me. Don't you forget it."

"Yeah," said Tom Beasley.

"Yeah," said Hidalgo.

"Yeah," said Pawnee.

"Now," said the preacher, "let's go back to the church and give thanks to the Lord."

Still waving the guns, they went out.

Pretty well cut up in my rear parts by that time, I signaled Cherokee to keep down. When finally we heard them stomp up the church steps, we slipped out the door and into the night and found our horses. As we made our way back up the hill, we could hear the voices rising behind us.

Praise be to God from whom all blessings flow

"Beautiful," Cherokee said. "Pure beauty."

No doubt about that. They might have been crazy by some standards, and they might have been desperadoes by others, but there was no doubting the beauty of their music or their faith.

I was still thinking about it—actually marveling at it—when we finally pulled up at a high spot of ground and looked back at Outlaw in the distance. The church lights were out now and the marshals and outlaws were probably on their cots and in their cells, sleeping the sleep of God-fearing men just returned from a purifying sermon. How, I wondered, could you deal with men like that? And then I wondered, how could God deal with men like that? Maybe that was why, in his uncertainty, he was letting them live so long.

Cherokee must have sensed my feelings. "I kind of feel like the Lord is on the other side's side," she said.

"He may be. You never can tell."

She was silent for a moment, and then she said, "Do you mind if I say a prayer?"

"Not if it fits."

"It fits."

I bowed my head.

"Keep us safe from harm and hurt," she said. "We're the good ones and they're the bad ones, and like that bad one just now said, don't you forget it."

"Amen," I said.

Then we rode into the night—two tired and hungry desperadoes runnin' from the "law."

11 ★ Nine Hundred Stolen Dollars

Cherokee and I made it, as the saying goes, through the night. We found a place in the hills where there was water and grass for the horses and good concealment for ourselves. After we had hung the damp saddle blankets over the rocks to dry, we ate a little hardtack and dried beef and then curled up against our saddles, using Will Jinks's shroud to guard against mosquitoes. I was just dozing off when I heard Cherokee say, "Territory, there's something I've got to ask."

"What is it?"

"What happened to your folks?"

"They got killed."

"How?"

"In the Run."

"You mean the Run of '93 . . . the Strip."

"Their wagon turned over and the horses ran away."

"You must have been pretty young."

"Two years old."

"They sure had pretty names. Who brought you up?"

"Nobody and everybody. Osages and old women mostly. Bitter Wells has got a lot of both."

"What are you gonna do when you're older?"

I was dozing off again, but I answered her honestly, saying, "Grow a long black mustache that droops at the corners." I didn't say anything about the tobacco stains, figuring she wouldn't much like that.

Then I went to sleep. And then I woke up, not certain why for a moment. Then I saw.

"Cherokee," I said.

"Huh."

She was asleep for sure.

"Your hair is in my mouth."

"It's too long," she said, without moving. "I'm gonna cut it when I get back home. My daddy says I'm beginning to look like a squaw."

"Your daddy's crazy," I said.

"Everybody knows that," she murmured. "That's why they call him ..."

I figured she was going to say "Crazy Ed" but I couldn't be sure, for she had gone back to sleep, the hair still there.

I did fall asleep then, for good. The next thing I knew, someone or something was snortin' in my face and the sun was high. It was Bullet Proof doin' the snortin'.

"He's nervous," Cherokee said, waking up too.

"You're right. I'll take a look."

I went up to the topmost rocks and looked down. At first I didn't see anything except the rimrocks far to the west and the Nescatunga to the south. It had gone down now and was running about normal. Then I saw something else passing through the cottonwoods down along the river. I motioned for Cherokee to come up.

"Down there," I said.

82

"Looks like a hearse."

"It is a hearse. Without a driver."

The hearse was black and the two horses pulling it were black, and everything else was proper and fittin' except for the missing driver. But maybe it wasn't so proper either, because nobody was leading it and nobody was following it and it was going a little too fast for dignity's sake, not to mention the comfort of the poor soul inside.

"They're runnin' away," Cherokee said. "Something must have spooked them."

"Hearse horses don't spook easy," I said. "And if they do, they usually head for the church or the cemetery."

"Still . . ." she said, but didn't finish. She didn't have to. I knew what she meant. And then she finished it. "Still, we've got to stop them. It's not proper to rush anyone to his grave like that."

We had to save another man in Goodbye Gulch, this time a dead one. "Maybe that's the way they do it in the gulch," I said. But I knew she was right, and already we were running back to our horses. Throwing on our saddles, along with the spade and the whisky and the shroud and the rest of it, we thundered down the slope to cut off the indecently hurrying horses.

It took us about two miles of hard riding to catch them. The hearse was bouncing over rocks and scraping trees as it careened along the trail to, I supposed, the cemetery. I got hold of the bridle bit and pulled them in, which wasn't hard to do, they being of a gentle kind, obedient to soft commands. You just naturally lowered your voice when you spoke to them, and they just naturally responded. Also they were old and gettin' tired. After I had pulled them in, they stood there with their heads down lookin' ashamed of themselves for their unseemly behavior.

Tyin' up the reins, I rode around to the back and got off Bullet Proof. As I walked away, he pushed me roughly with his head, as if to say, "See how fast I am," which seemed to me to be needless bragging on his part, since almost any horse could outrun a hearse horse, especially one with a loaded hearse. Cherokee was already off and opening the rear doors. We stuck our heads in. The curtains were drawn and for a moment we couldn't make out anything. A jagged hole in the roof let a little sunlight through, which I figured was done that way deliberately to create halos on the passenger. Then, rising up from out of a big box came first an old weather-beaten hat, then some whiskers, then about half of the rest of him, and then finally the shotgun.

"Don't move," old man Sheldon said. "My finger's on the trigger."

His finger was always on the trigger. It looked like he intended to go through Heaven with his finger on the trigger. God himself would probably have a problem gettin' that finger off the trigger.

God might have another problem too, I saw right off, if old man Sheldon went to the Promised Land. He was stuck in the box. Looked like somebody had stuffed him in. And that jagged hole in the top of the hearse looked like it had been made by a shotgun blast.

Recognizing us, he said, "They thought I was dead. You got a drink?"

We were still looking straight at the shotgun. "Did you fire both barrels through the roof or just one?" I asked.

"Hee! Hee! Both," he said, real proud. "I always fire both. Got to fire both. My finger won't fire one at a time. Hee! Hee!"

"Then I reckon we don't have to be afraid of the gun."

"Oh, my, no," he said, real gently. "You're my friends." And then, "Would you kindly help me out of this box?"

"Who put you in there?" Cherokee asked, as we climbed into the hearse and started tryin' to pry him loose.

"Don't rightly know. Somebody musta made a mistake. Somebody's always doin' that, tryin' to cart me off." He made an effort, gruntin' a little, but he was stuck good, and he wouldn't—or maybe couldn't—put down that shotgun. "I was asleep. Guess they figured I was dead." He grunted again, as if that would help us to pull him out, but it didn't. "It was probably Dick Creel and Tom Beasley," he grunted. "More'n likely they found me when they made the dawn patrol. They want my gold mine, you know. Also they want to shut my mouth. They're afraid that on my deathbed I will tell my secrets, and that will ruin their lives . . . and," he added, "most of all it will ruin their dreams. Crazy men have dreams too, you know. In fact, these ain't got much else." Still gruntin', me on one side of him and Cherokee on the other and the shotgun in the middle, he said, "Don't intend to let them get my gold mine. Intend to leave it to the church. Been gettin' me a powerful feelin' for religion lately."

Cherokee stopped pryin' at him long enough to pat him on the hand that held the shotgun, saying, "That's real nice, Mr. Sheldon. The church needs money to save the souls of men like Dick Creel and Tom Beasley."

I put my shoulder against him and pushed, but he wouldn't budge. Something creaked a little, though I couldn't tell if it was him or the box or the hearse.

"Yes, ma'am," he said, gruntin' and using the shotgun like an oar in a boat, "they do sin pretty good, I guess. Still, I don't exactly trust the preacher either." Then, puffing and wheezing, he said, "Don't think we can make it. Maybe you just better leave me. Don't want to be no bother. Your lives are in danger, you know." He was still scraping like an oar with the shotgun.

"You're no bother, Mr. Sheldon," Cherokee said.

"That's mighty kind of you, ma'am," he said, rowing away.

"I'm countin' on you to make your mark and clear my daddy's name."

He stopped rowing. "I took an oath, ma'am."

"Let's slide the box out," I said. I was gettin' up a sweat.

"Good idea," old man Sheldon said. "Then you can just turn it over and I'll fall out. Take care my gun don't get dirty."

It wasn't quite as easy as he made it sound, but we finally got the box out—dropping it about four feet to the ground—and him out of it. There wasn't much left . . . of the box, that is.

"Now I've got to reload," he said, as soon as he hit the ground. Then he started trying to get his finger uncurled from the trigger.

When he finally got it uncurled and was fumbling in

his tattered clothing for more cartridges, I said, "As long as you've got your finger free, why don't you sign the confession? Then we can make a run for it. The river's down."

"You'd never make it," he said, sliding the cartridges in and snapping the shotgun shut. "The marshals are everywhere. They're out to get you. Heard 'em say so. And nobody gets out of here alive if they don't want 'em to. Don't know how you've kept alive so far. And besides, I can't break my oath until I'm on my deathbed. 'Twouldn't be proper."

"That's right," Cherokee said. " 'Twouldn't be. But it would clear a man's name."

"And it would dirty another man's."

"But if it's the truth and if he deserves it," she said, "isn't that better for everybody?"

"Ordinarily 'twould be," he said. He had the finger back in place now around the trigger of the loaded gun. Made him a lot more sure of himself. You could even hear the difference in his voice. "But this part of the world ain't ordinary. Actually it ain't even part of the world. Nobody wants it, 'cept outlaws. Oklahoma don't want it. Texas don't want it. Even the Indians don't want it. The men here ain't ordinary, the laws sure ain't ordinary, the customs ain't ordinary, the climate ain't even ordinary. The good Lord himself knows the place ain't ordinary, and I suppose he's allowed for that, though I don't know how he's ever gonna separate the good men from the bad ones unless he just pronounces everybody crazy and sends them to some special place. When you've got outlaws that used to be marshals, and marshals that used to be outlaws, and in between times some of them was preachers, then I doubt if even the good Lord can tell who deserves a good name and who deserves a bad one. Say," he said, lookin' up at me, "you ain't got any more of that whisky, have you?"

"Sure," I said.

For some reason Cherokee didn't object. So old man Sheldon took a snort, wiped his whiskers with the back of the hand that held the bottle, then took another one, and said, "Well, now, that's better." Then he paused and shook his head. "But it don't make that box look any prettier." He was standing with one foot in the coffin, the shotgun under his arm, the bottle still in his hand. Looked like a painting that might have been called "Old Man Sheldon's Last Stand." It wasn't until he had almost emptied the bottle that he managed to get his foot out of the box, so I guessed Doc was right and the stuff really was keepin' him alive.

"You want us to help you back to your diggin's?" Cherokee asked.

"No. You've got too many troubles already." He scratched his head for a moment, thoughtfully, through a hole in the battered hat. "In fact," he said, "I almost forgot. They paid your ransom money."

She looked at me. I looked at her. What now had happened in that unordinary place? "Who paid?" I asked.

"Young fellow. 'Bout your age. 'Cept he was an Osage."

"Clyde Blood!" I said, remembering the marshal's words about keeping both eyes on your friends, and remembering too that never, never, never do you know what's goin' through an Osage Indian's head.

"I overheard 'em talkin'," old man Sheldon said, "when I woke up in the box, so I peeked through the curtains. The young Indian was ridin' a pinto. He gave nine sacks of money to Dick Creel. Then Dick Creel made a speech about bein' friends with the Osages for as long as grass growed. Pretty sorry speech, to tell you the truth."

"What else did the Osage say?"

"Said there was a hundred dollars in each sack and that it was for your safe return. He said he was your best friend. Oh, yes, I almost forgot. I believe he said he robbed the bank to get the money, though I couldn't be sure about that because that was where I shot the hole in the roof and horses spooked and the driver fell off and then you came along."

I knew in my heart it was true. Clyde Blood had robbed the bank at Bitter Wells. Somehow even that seemed fittin' and proper here, bein' as it was illegal.

"Who's Clyde Blood?" Cherokee asked.

"A bank robber friend of mine."

"He shouldn't have done it," old man Sheldon said.

"He sure shouldn't," Cherokee said. "It's against the law."

"Didn't mean that," Sheldon said. "Meant that now Dick Creel will just ask for more. That friend of yours is sure going to have to rob a lot of banks to satisfy Dick Creel. He likes money. And you two are liable to be runnin' for the rest of your lives."

Old man Sheldon was limberin' up his legs a little, shufflin' down the trail. Cherokee and I were back on our horses again, ready to ride . . . for what began to look like the rest of our lives. I gave the hearse horses a little more rein and they started off in a slow and dignified walk toward what I guessed was the graveyard. The box was still in the middle of the trail.

After a few uncertain steps—partly due to drink and partly due to age—old man Sheldon turned around and said, "There's something else I ought to tell you. Dick Creel and the marshals keep their stolen money in the basement under the jail. There's a trap door in the middle of the room." He chuckled pleasantly, the shotgun going up and down. "Knowin' you two," he said, "I figure you'll try to get the money back and return it to its rightful owners."

"I figure you're right," I said.

"My, my," he said. "You sure are pure."

"I figure you're right again," Cherokee said.

Then we waved goodbye to what had begun to seem not only the best but the only friend we had in Goodbye Gulch . . . if you didn't count Clyde Blood.

Just as we turned away, Cherokee pointed into the distance across the river and said, "Look! What's going on?"

Over on the other bank a great throng of men and horses had come to a stop at the crossing. Now they sat looking across the river at Goodbye Gulch.

"I don't know," I said, "but I've got a feeling it's a posse. Let's take cover."

We pulled in behind the rocks.

12 ★ The Great Standoff

It was a sight to see. Also it was enough to make you weep. On one side of the river was the posse, about a hundred strong, and on the other side was what Dick Creel would probably have called his "point man"—a lone rider out front to alert the main force strung out behind him. From where we were I had no trouble identifying the posse. It was from Bitter Wells, led by Sheriff Boggs and his deputy, who, you could tell even from a distance, was drunk. You could also see that none of them—drunk or sober—were very anxious to cross the river. When they had drawn themselves up in a line along the bank, Sheriff Boggs tied what looked like a white bed sheet to a fishing pole and held it high in the air. Looked like the flag of permanent surrender.

"They sure give up easy," Cherokee said.

"They wanta parley. That means they'd like to get what they came for without gettin' shot."

"Maybe they came to get us back. Judge Docker sends out posses all the time to help humans in distress."

"Don't think so." I didn't tell her that what they had come to get back—bein' money instead of humans—

would probably have made her Judge Docker weep Choctaw tears—if he had any left—for the white man's ways.

"Dick Creel and the marshals are moving forward," she said, "with Tom Beasley and the outlaws backing them up."

"Yes, and there's Dead Shot Steel with his Bible in his hand."

"Maybe they'll sing the song," she said.

"What song?"

" 'We Shall Gather by the River.' "

"Fittin' and proper," I said. "That's exactly what they're doin'. They're gonna gather by the river and speak of stolen money."

I guessed I was gettin' a little crazy, the way you do when you've just pried a live man out of a coffin and then been told that your best friend has robbed a bank to ransom you and then find yourself watching what looks like an armed congregation of ancient sinners gettin' ready to make their last stand. Wouldn't have surprised me at all if they had started out by singing.

But they didn't. Instead, approaching the river on the signal of his point man, Dick Creel drew up his ancient marshals on their ancient horses in a real U.S. government-approved formation. In back of them Tom Beasley and his ancient outlaws slouched on their horses, spittin' now and then and looking slovenly. Across the river the white flag fluttered. You had to admit, there was a certain touch of color about it all. If you had been ninety years old and watching it and not known that the two warring parties were going to fight it out over nine hundred stolen dollars, it might even have been beautiful. As it was, it was just kind of pitiful and comic and sad, and the sorrow you felt was mostly for the horses, they being innocent participants.

Everybody was wearing guns, but only the outlaws actually had their hands resting on the butts. The way they slouched in the saddle, it was probably more comfortable that way. Kind of helped to hold them up. Dick Creel and the marshals—being men of honor and respecters of tradition—kept their gloved hands out in the open. They knew all the niceties of the ceremony. As did Sheriff Boggs, being an old lawman himself. He held the white flag firmly, his right hand raised in a gesture of peace. If the deputy didn't forget himself and reach for his bottle and draw gunfire from the opposite shore, they probably wouldn't violate the sacred principles of the parley by shedding blood. Also they were all at a pretty safe distance from each other, considering the uncertainties of their hands and the dimness of their eyes.

When Chief Marshal Creel had taken up his position, Marshals Gerhart and Tinklehoff cantered forward to his side. The old horses didn't canter too well, but they got there. They were followed by Fats Tubstyle and Hector Grunt. Apparently old Grunt's horse had found his way home after all.

"What's Grunt doin' there?" Cherokee asked. "He's not a marshal."

"Just likes to act like one," I explained. "Grunt's what you call an aide-de-camp. That's a flunky. Swabs out the cells and scoops manure from the stalls. You remember how he smelled."

"I sure do."

Marshal Tinklehoff raised his gauntleted hand and cried across the river, "Marshal Creel presents his compliments and has the honor to request the nature of your business."

The sheriff jiggled the white flag and cried back, "We've come for our money, unlawfully took from the coffers of the bank."

"Means it was stolen," I said.

"Sure a funny way to say it."

"They're government officials," I explained.

"Judge Docker doesn't talk like that."

"He's a Choctaw."

The marshals conferred, seriously and long. Then they reassumed formation and Marshal Tinklehoff raised his gauntleted hand again. "Marshal Creel begs me to inform you that the money in question was legally tendered to his jurisdiction for payment of services rendered. Therefore, we have no choice but to resist if you attack and to arrest you if you persist."

The sheriff and his posse conferred, the deputy seizing the opportunity to sneak a drink. Then Sheriff Boggs jiggled the bed sheet again and cried, "We've got you outnumbered."

The marshals conferred. Then Marshal Tinklehoff rode forward and cried, "Be so courteous as to permit us to send for reinforcements."

That must have seemed a reasonable request, for Sheriff Boggs jiggled the bed sheet to show that he respected it. Immediately the marshals dispatched a rider over the hill toward Outlaw. Then Reverend Dead Shot Steel rode forward and said, "Let us pray. If we fall in battle, our mothers will be grieved."

Their mothers would have had to be a hundred and thirty years old . . . well beyond grieving. But nobody seemed to notice that. The outlaws, at the mention of their mothers, took off their hats, being, though very mean, very devout. The marshals couldn't remove their hats because they were on duty. The old horses were already standing with their heads down, looking like they were constantly at prayer, which maybe they were, knowing as they probably did the follies of their masters. On the other side the white bed sheet was dipped just slightly, and the only thing you could hear was the river flowing and Dead Shot Steel praying.

About the time the prayer was over, the reinforcements arrived . . . around a hundred of them.

"It's going to be a standoff," I said.

"How do you know?"

"The sides are equal, and there's a river between them."

"That means they might be here all day," she said.

"Maybe all night too. And it also means that there's nobody left in Outlaw. We can get the nine hundred dollars back right now."

"They probably left a guard."

"We'll overpower him."

"I'd like that."

I knew she would. We let the parleying ceremony get started good, with lots of conferring and flag-jiggling, then we slipped up the ravine and kept to the cover of the hills until we were out of sight. After that the going was easy. We rode straight into Outlaw, down what was left of what was called Sunset Street. Seemed a perfect name.

Except for a few dogs, which didn't seem to mind our presence, nobody greeted us. Riding around to the back of the jail, we slipped off our horses and went inside. It looked deserted. Even sounded deserted. Then from one of the cells we heard a noise. Sounded like somebody with a bad case of asthma. Actually it sounded more like a cow with a bad case of asthma. Breathin' awful hard. Chokin' hard too. Sounded just like a dyin' cow.

"There he is," Cherokee said. "In the back cell."

I couldn't quite believe what I saw. Whoever he was, he must have been a real desperado, the kind you couldn't afford to take any chances with. He was not only tied up and locked in, but he also had about half a horse blanket stuffed in his mouth. The only normal thing about him was, he was wearin' two guns. You couldn't tell what he was saying or trying to. The only thing you could really say for sure about him was that he was almost a goner. That was clear from the color of his face, a very dark blue.

"We've got to save him," Cherokee said. "He can't last much longer."

"You're right," I said. "It's the human thing to do." By this time I was resigned to saving every dying man in Goodbye Gulch for something or another.

"He won't be grateful," Cherokee said. "You can tell by looking at him. But we've got to save his life anyway."

"That's right," I said. Then, remembering Dead Shot Steel's prayer by the river, I added, "He may have a mother somewhere."

Gettin' to him was a problem. The cell was locked and the keys weren't there. And we had to get to him fast too, otherwise we'd be lookin' through the bars at a body with a horse blanket in its mouth.

"He's gettin' bluer in the face," Cherokee said.

I got down on my knees, jabbin' myself a little in the backside with my spurs, and reached inside the cell, tryin' for the edge of the horse blanket. I was stretchin' and gruntin' and the guy was gaggin' and snortin' and lookin' wild-eyed and Cherokee was sayin', "Stretch, Territory, stretch."

"Push me," I grunted.

She almost broke my neck. I thought my head was goin' through the bars to the other side. But I got the edge of the blanket. And then I got another jab from my spurs as I bent back and pulled the blanket with me. By now I figured I was bleedin' steady back there.

"It's not comin' out," Cherokee said.

She was right. The blanket wouldn't come out. Instead, as we pulled on it, the desperado came scraping across the floor, his face bluer and bluer around the gills. I was beginning to worry.

"Reach through the bars and get a finger in the side of his mouth," I said. "It'll stretch."

She looked at me and then at the purple face. "He'll bite," she said. "I can see his teeth." She was down with her head almost against the floor, lookin' up at his mouth.

"If he's got teeth, he's not a marshal," I said. "Probably the jailer."

She had to push, but she got the finger in, stretchin' his mouth up almost to his eyes. And then, bit by bit, the blanket began to give. When it finally came, I fell backwards hard, tearing myself up some more, and the guy's head plopped down against the floor. He was weak but he was alive. It took him a while to get his color back, and a little longer for him to lift his head. When he did, he kind of slobbered and said, "I'll git you for this." Looking up at us with accusing eyes, he said, "That horse blanket was filthy."

"Yeah," I said, "the horse probably had saddle sores. Who did it, Bluegills?" Seemed a proper name for him.

"I didn't see who did it. Took me from behind. But I figure it was you two. Then you got scared and came back."

"Told you he wouldn't be grateful," Cherokee said.

"You gonna untie me now?" he grunted.

"We already saved your life," Cherokee said.

"And besides," I added, "you're probably wanted for something."

"How'd you know?" he asked, lookin' up in surprise.

"Was it you that shot the tax collector?" Cherokee asked real fast.

"Ah, no, ma'am."

"Who was it?"

"Can't tell you, ma'am. Took an oath. My lips are sealed." He smacked his mouth shut to show us how his lips were sealed.

Everybody's lips were sealed. I knew we weren't going to get any information from him. So I took the slobbery horse blanket, stuffed it through the bars, opened it, and let it fall over his face.

"That'll keep the flies off, Bluegills."

"Thanks," he mumbled from underneath. It sounded like he meant it.

We found the trap door in the middle of the room and went down the ladder into the darkness. It took our eyes a while to get used to things, but finally we made out what looked like sacks of money that had recently been put there.

"Those must be the ones," I said.

"That's right. There are nine of them."

I gathered up five sacks and Cherokee got four, and then we rattled back up the ladder, coins clinking heavily against the rungs. Outside, we stashed the loot in our saddlebags and headed for the hills. Outlaw, except for the stray dogs, was still deserted.

We had ridden about two miles and were moving along a brushy ravine when a figure kind of rose up out of nowhere—seemin' to come out of the earth and the rocks—right in front of us. He had even taken Bullet Proof by surprise.

"I stole the money back," Clyde Blood said, with that expression on his face which was not an expression. "It's there on that rock."

Nine sacks stood neatly stacked on the rock. On the outside was written: TERRITORIAL BANK OF BITTER WELLS.

I looked at Cherokee.

She looked at me.

Clyde Blood looked at both of us.

I think the horses even looked at one another, as if to ask what I asked, "Then what have we got here?"

Cherokee pulled out a sack and held it up. On the outside were the words: PAYROLL SANTA FE RWY. Then I pulled out a sack and held it up. The words read: COLLECTION PLATE METHODIST CHURCH.

Silence. Nothing but silence. I said nothing. Cherokee said nothing. The horses stood in what seemed silent sympathy. Finally Clyde Blood said, "You're in real trouble now. I don't just mean with the authorities. I mean with God himself."

I wanted to tell him that he was going to be in trouble too, for helping us that way, but when I looked up he was gone. Just disappeared.

The nine sacks still stood neatly on the rock.

13 ★ Unwanted Money

There was something else on that rock too—the keys to the jail cells, on a big brass ring. When Clyde Blood looted a jail, he believed in doing it right. Tie up the jailer, stuff a horse blanket in his mouth, lock him in the cell, and steal the keys. All without being seen. You had to admire his ability even if you didn't approve of what he was doing. That was a grand total of one bank and one jail he had robbed in the space of two days, without being seen . . . I hoped.

"That boy's gonna get in trouble someday," Cherokee said, "if he's not careful."

"He's very careful," I said.

"I think he means well, but . . ."

"But what?"

"He made things worse."

"He always does." And then I added, "We're still alive."

That made her smile through the mud and grime and streaks of sweat adorning her pretty face. Both of us were filthy, both of us were tired, both of us were hungry, and both of us knew without even having to say it that we weren't going to leave Goodbye Gulch until we had old man Sheldon's mark on that confession. The money might complicate things a little, but it wasn't going to defeat us. In fact, nothing was going to defeat us—hunger, money, or anything else. Somewhere, without even knowing it, we had reached a point where there could be no turning back. With me it was no longer so much a case of saving the reputation of a man—who probably didn't care about it one way or the other, no matter how his daughter felt—as it was of winning a ridiculously human and dangerous game . . . what old Geoffrey Tolliver would have called standing your ground and sticking by your guns and not letting yourself be buffaloed and several other things meaning you had to be staunch and true to the bitter end. Also, he probably would have told us to put our faith in the Lord, but since it looked like we had filched some of the Lord's money it didn't seem proper to be pushing for favors right then.

We stacked our sacks of money on the rock alongside the others. Made quite a heap. Some of it was gold and some of it was silver. Felt real good to the touch. Pretty too . . . the dollars with eagles on them.

We looked at each other across the sacks of stolen loot. "What do we do with it?" I asked.

"We can't keep it. It's not ours."

Simple and beautiful words. Amazing Grace. How sweet the sound. *We can't keep it. It's not ours.* It's a wonder the jack rabbits didn't look up in surprise. In that place and at that time, sacks of money floating around were regarded as gifts from heaven. For sure they were to be kept, at least until the sheriff came looking for them, and then they were to be defended. It had been that way since the time of the conquistadors. The gold you found—in no matter what form—was yours.

"You're right," I said. "We can't keep it. It's not ours." I couldn't get those simple words out of my mind. They were too beautiful, too true. Made the air around you fresher, cleaner. The fact that they were spoken by a Cherokee, about white men's money, may have been the cause of my marveling. For I couldn't keep from thinking that, by the same token, any honest white man should have been able to say the same thing about the Oklahoma Territory. "We can't keep it. It's not ours." And if you wanted to press things a little, a truly honest white man should have been able to say the same thing about the entire continent. "We can't keep it. It's not ours."

"We could bury it," I said, "for the time being. Or better yet . . ." But then I paused.

"Better what?"

"Do you trust old man Sheldon?"

She looked at me across the sacks of gold and silver and finally she said, "Sure. Don't you?"

"Yes," I said. "But I have been known to misjudge men. Maybe because I started young and always gave them the benefit of the doubt."

"We can trust old man Sheldon," she said. "He'll hide it good and never touch it."

I was curious. "How can you be so sure? It's a lot of money. Eighteen sacks of gold and silver."

"He's not interested in money. He's not even digging for gold any more. He's digging for lost dreams."

Digging for lost dreams. Amazing words. How sweet

103

the sound. I wished I had said them myself. I looked at her across the sacks of gold and silver, thinking, "I am always looking at her across sacks of gold and silver or the barrels of loaded shotguns or the bodies of half-dead desperadoes with ropes around their necks or horse blankets in their mouths. And always when I look, I wonder if I'll ever see her any other way. But most of all I marvel at what comes tumbling from her lips."

"I think you're right," I said. "Let's load up. We'll take it to the cave after dark."

"Suppose I'm wrong," she said.

Digging for lost dreams? "You couldn't be," I said, tying on the sacks as she handed them to me. "And even if you are, any man that digs for dreams for fifty years deserves something."

She smiled at me across the saddle, now almost covered with the loot, the spade, the whisky and the shroud. "How about the marshals?" she asked. "And the outlaws? Aren't they chasing things that don't exist . . . dreams? Don't they deserve something?"

"There's a difference. They're chasing them with guns in their hands and I don't know what in their hearts."

She smiled at me. "They know," she said.

I wondered.

When we had lashed everything down, we ate the last of the dried beef and hardtack and drank the last of the water in the canteen. The sun was just going down when we started moving in the direction of old man Sheldon's diggin's, keeping to the ravines.

I couldn't resist peeping over the hill to see if the great standoff was still going on down by the Nescatunga.

It was. But now it was a very small standoff, the night guard, as Dick Creel probably would have called it. Only one campfire burned on each side of the river. The main force had pulled back.

"That means the marshals and the outlaws are back at the jail," I said. "Dick Creel's probably plotting his strategy for tomorrow."

But as we skirted the hills above Outlaw and saw the kerosene lamp burning in the window of the jail, we knew that something was wrong. The lamp was turned down low. The jail was too quiet. There was no movement of marshals or outlaws.

"Something's wrong down there," Cherokee said.

"Something sure is."

I turned Bullet Proof in the direction of the town. He snorted softly, meaning that it was as safe as a warm barn in winter. "Let's take a look," I said.

With the coins chinking in the sacks, we walked the horses slowly down the slope, coming up behind the jail to the window where the kerosene lamp was burning. The jail was empty, except for Bluegills. He was sleeping on the floor of the locked cell. Even from outside you could hear him snoring. Behind us the church was silent and dark.

"Something's wrong, real wrong," I said. "You still got Fats's gun?"

"Sure have."

"Bring it along and keep it aimed at Bluegills. I figure it's the only language he understands."

I took the keys and Cherokee took the gun and we slid from our saddles and slipped in through the back door. Bluegills slept on, the blanket over him rising and falling with his snores. I rattled the cell door. The snoring stopped and Bluegills looked up from under his hat brim. Cherokee pointed the gun through the bars.

"Where is everybody?" I asked.

A sly light came into Bluegills's eyes. "Will you let me out if I tell you?"

I put the key in the lock without turning it. "Where?" I asked again.

Bluegills got up and started over, the horse blanket hanging from his shoulders. That was when I noticed that somehow he had got his hands untied. He was still holding them behind him, pretending that they were tied, but you could see they weren't. He kept coming slowly, that sly look in his eyes.

"That's far enough," Cherokee said.

"Where?" I asked again.

Bluegills hesitated, as if maybe thinking about trying for his guns.

"Don't," I said, "or we'll wrap you in the last horse blanket of your life."

That seemed to change his mind. "Sure you'll let me out?" he said. "I gotta go to the backhouse."

"As soon as you tell me where they are."

"Up at the diggin's. Old man Sheldon's on his death-bed . . . for sure this time."

"How do you know?"

" 'Cause he ain't callin' for whisky."

I turned the key. Bluegills slouched out of the cell and started for the door. Cherokee turned with him, the gun steady in her hand.

"Don't go near the horses," I said, "or that blue one will kill you."

"Not if I kill him first."

"Hold it!" I shouted.

Cherokee cocked the gun. Bluegills stopped. I went over and took both his pistols, tossing them back inside the cell and locking the door again and tossing the keys in after them.

"I wouldn'ta done it," Bluegills said.

"I don't believe you," I said. "You'd do anything. Now do me a favor and get out of sight."

He disappeared through the door, still trailing the horse blanket.

"You know something?" Cherokee said.

"What?"

"This gun isn't even loaded."

"Keep it a secret," I said. "I've got a feelin' we may have to rely on it again."

"You know," she said, "I've got the same feelin'."

14 * Scratching Out the Truth

We knew what we had to do. Everything had suddenly become simple. We had to reach old man Sheldon in time to hear his dying words and guide his dying hand. It was as simple as that. And we had to get through nine renegade marshals and a pack of outlaws to do it. Simple. But before we did anything, we had to unburden ourselves and our horses of the load. If the time came when we had to make a run for it, I didn't want any extra weight holdin' us back. Might make the difference between living and dying. And certainly I wasn't going to ask a horse like Bullet Proof to get caught, shot, harmed or hurt because of needless baggage.

I pulled the nine sacks belonging to the Methodist Church and the Santa Fe Railway off the saddles and set them on the church steps right in front of the door. Then I took down the spade and the lugs of whisky and the false teeth and spectacles and set them down too, tossing the shroud over everything. It seemed, even in my haste, a fitting final touch.

"That preacher will probably drink the whisky," Cherokee said.

"And steal the money too. But that's all right. It's rotgut whisky and blood money."

"Some of it belongs to the Lord," she said.

"Yes, and only the Lord himself probably knows where it came from."

We can't keep it. It's not ours.

"What do we do with the sacks from Bitter Wells?" she asked.

"I'll stuff them in my saddlebags. At least we know who they belong to." While I was stuffing, I noticed the hymnbook. "What do we do with this? I don't think we'll have much time for singing."

"I'll take it," she said, "to put the confession in. That'll keep it nice and neat."

Then we were in the saddle, headed for the diggin's and the wildest night of our lives. Even the horses seemed to sense that we were coming up to the show-down—from which if you are lucky you walk away and if you're not you don't. Simple as that. Bullet Proof was pulling hard against the reins, frothing a little, grinding at the bit as if to say he could chew it up and swallow it if he wanted to. And though I couldn't see it in the dark, I knew he had that murderous glint in his eye. Cherokee rode beside me, a small piece of paper fluttering in her hand. She had the confession ready.

At the entrance to the canyon leading down to the diggin's, I pulled to a stop. Farther down, outside the cave dug in the side of the hill, you could just make out the bunched forms of horses. Over them an occasional bit of light shone, as if someone inside had passed between them and a lantern.

"Cherokee," I said, "there are a thousand tricks we could use to fool the marshals and the outlaws, but we're not going to use them. Time's too short, we're both too tired, and I'm especially weary of dealing with crazy men. Instead, we're going to do it all straight and clean. If we win, we win. If we lose, we lose."

"I guess you'd call it shootin' the moon," she said.

"I guess you would," I said. "Just remember this. Keep close to old man Sheldon, 'cause I've got a feelin' he's on our side, and I know for sure that—dead or alive—his finger will be curled around the trigger of that shotgun. If there's one thing in this place you can count on, it's that."

"It's a pity he can't die in peace," she said.

"He'd rather die this way," I said. "Probably been dreamin' about it all his lonely life. You get lots of attention when you've got lots of secrets, especially when the secrets have something to do with gold. Ready?"

"Ready."

"Let's go."

We rode slowly the last hundred yards, taking no precautions, in no hurry. It's amazing how easy everything becomes when you've decided to shoot the moon. Nor did we stop or even hesitate at the entrance to the cave. Just rode on in, slowly, surely, calmly, as if in the habit of riding into the diggin's of dying prospectors every night about that time. I even managed to speak quietly and casually when I said, "Evenin' everyone."

However many guns turned in our direction would be hard to say, since I wasn't countin'. First there were the slouching outlaws, all with drawn guns, and a little beyond them the gauntleted and toothless marshals in a row as if in church, their guns drawn too. Over against the wall, sitting on the gunpowder keg, old man Sheldon held his shotgun kind of carelessly, pointin' it in the general direction of the dynamite. Everybody seemed to be holding a gun on everybody else, and for the moment all the guns seemed to be turned toward us.

Dick Creel stepped forward, flanked by Gerhart and Tinklehoff. "In the name of the law," he said, "you're under arrest."

"You got it all wrong, Creel," I said. "And I mean all." Close up he was a sight to see. Toothless, half blind, a crazy look of determination on his face.

"I'm still the law here," he said. "Lift your hands and throw down your guns."

"Sorry, Creel. It's a little late for that."

Old man Sheldon wiggled his shotgun slightly and said, "Back off, Creel. Them's my friends. They're runnin' from the law."

It was no use to protest now. Since old man Sheldon had made up his mind we were runnin' from the law, we were runnin' from the law. And did it really matter now?

"They're under arrest," Dick Creel said. "I'm takin' 'em in."

He really meant it. His crazy eyes lit up like burning coals when he said, "I'm takin' 'em in."

"Back off," old man Sheldon said. And then he chuckled, pleasantly, amused not at the guns or even at Dick Creel but at something far more sane. "That horse's doin' it again," he said.

"It's the guns," I said. "They make him nervous." I

nodded to Cherokee. We got down, slowly, casually. The guns turned with us as we walked in front of the slouching outlaws and the gauntleted marshals to the keg where old man Sheldon sat. Behind us one of the outlaws made an attempt to inspect our saddlebags, and Bullet Proof spun him backwards head over heels against the wall, where he lay tangled in his spurs.

"That horse will kill anyone who goes close to him," I said.

"Old Grunt was right," one of the outlaws said. "A killer horse."

That was when I noticed that Grunt wasn't there. Neither was Fats Tubstyle. The rest of the marshals stood in a row, their guns turned back toward old man Sheldon, as did the slouching outlaws, Tom Beasley at their head. Old man Sheldon kept his shotgun pointed at the dynamite across the way, his finger on the trigger. Cherokee was on one side of him and I was on the other.

"Glad you came," he said. "You got the paper?"

Cherokee laid it on the gun barrel, just ahead of the hammers, and held out the fountain pen.

"Don't know how I'm gonna do this, ma'am," he said. "Cain't take my finger off the trigger. I don't trust any of them . . . not even the preacher."

I hadn't noticed the preacher before, standin' a little to one side, a gun in one hand, the Bible in the other, ready to use whichever he needed first.

"Give me your left hand," Cherokee said. "I'll guide it so you can make your mark."

Keeping the right hand on the trigger, and the stock of the gun against him, old man Sheldon took the fountain pen in his left hand. The shotgun bobbed up and down as Cherokee helped him make his mark on the paper. The guns in the cave seemed to get a little tenser as the pen scratched and the gun barrel bobbed.

"You're stealin' his gold," Dick Creel said. "Makin' him sign away his rights."

"I'm clearin' my daddy's name," Cherokee said, looking up and straight into the guns. "This mark says my daddy didn't shoot the tax collector."

The slouching outlaws and the gauntleted marshals seemed to draw back in hushed surprise at the words. Then their voices seemed to come out in a chorus. "You took an oath, Sheldon. You gave your sacred word."

"Back off, all of you. I'm a dyin' man. Got to lift the burdens from my soul."

"Amen," the preacher said, tapping the Bible with the gun.

Now Cherokee was guiding old man Sheldon's hand down to the other corner of the paper. That was where she was supposed to write the name of the man that shot the tax collector. I had a feeling this might bring the cave crashing down around our ears, especially if in telling her the name, old man Sheldon spoke the words too loud. You could feel the nervousness behind the pointed guns.

"Some things is better left buried," Dick Creel said. His voice had grown softer.

"Back off, Dick Creel. I aim to rest in peace. I know the truth and you know the truth, and every outlaw in this cave knows the truth. The difference is, I'm a little closer to dyin' than the rest of you. Not much, but still a little." He laughed softly, the gun bobbin'. "Somehow, it's all beginnin' to git a little funny. So, back off, Dick Creel."

I looked at Dick Creel. Something—it was hard to say what—was burning, almost blazing, deep inside him. You could see it in the way he held his crazy head aloft. In his bearing, and maybe even in his spirit, he was still a U.S. marshal. Renegade, but still a marshal. Gone bad, long ago, but still a marshal. As were the rest of them. Renegades, but still going through the motions. And the outlaws too. Nothing left for them to loot any more, but still going through the motions. And the preacher too, going through the motions with a gun in one hand and the Bible in the other, sayin', "Amen," and fingerin' the trigger.

"I ain't backin' off," Dick Creel said. "I've come close to dyin' many times, and it ain't the least bit funny."

"You want me to take my secret with me," old man Sheldon said.

"I want you to honor your oath," Creel said.

Somewhere the conversation had taken a turn in tone. Now the pathetic old prospector and the ridiculous old marshal seemed neither pathetic nor ridiculous. A quiet dignity had crept in unnoticed. Even their silences seemed to have meaning. There was something—the secret, I guessed—between them, and their words seemed as deadly and serious as the guns they were pointin' at each other. Cherokee was still holding old man Sheldon's hand, and old man Sheldon was still holding the fountain pen. Puzzled by the change in tone, we looked across the shotgun at each other.

"You don't want me to ruin any reputations," old man Sheldon said. "You're forgettin' that this girl's daddy is wrongfully accused. You know it. I know it."

"He can live with it," Dick Creel said. "Men have lived with worse."

Cherokee and I frowned across the gun. There was some meaning here that we weren't getting. You could tell it by the softness of their words.

"This girl's sincere," old man Sheldon said.

"I'm sincere too," Dick Creel said.

And he was. You could see it, sense it, feel it. So were the other marshals. So even were the outlaws and the preacher, who said, "Amen," again in the silence that now hung. Men gone wrong, all of them, but sincere. Crazy men, too, but still sincere. What I couldn't figure out was why they, who had no reputations to protect, were so sincere.

"Guide my hand, young lady," old man Sheldon said. "The pen's a-gittin' heavy."

He could hold the shotgun with no trouble, but the pen weighed him down.

"Leave it buried," Dick Creel said. "The world will be a better place."

"Amen," said the preacher.

Cherokee looked up at Dick Creel. "Do you mean that?"

"I sure do, ma'am." He took off his hat, a marshal to the end—renegade, but a marshal. His long gray mustache drooped forlornly. "It's about the only thing I do believe. Everything else in this world just kind of"—he waved his hand with the gun in it—"got away."

115

"You went bad, Creel," old man Sheldon said. "You were a U.S. marshal and a good one, but you went bad."

"I went back and forth like all the rest of them."

Sheldon was looking at him straight now, the gun not bobbing. The next words were soft and, at least to Cherokee and me, totally mysterious. "Back and forth? Not quite. We're talkin' about an outlaw . . ."

". . . the best," Tom Beasley interrupted. "One of the best that ever rode . . ."

". . . who," Sheldon went on, "went good."

"The best there too," Creel said. "So leave it there. Leave it buried." He paused, looking awfully old and awfully sad. "You've got to believe in someone. So long as there's just one person to put your faith in, everything's all right. But there's got to be one."

"I'm puttin' my faith in God," old man Sheldon said, "and in the truth. Guide my hand, young lady. Scratch it out slow. 'Cause to tell you the truth, it even pains me a little to put it down." He paused. "Believe I'll whisper it to you, if you don't mind."

But the aches and pains of time had cramped him hard around the shoulders, and he couldn't reach her ear. Seemed, however, he could turn his burly whiskers in my direction, so fate laid that one down on me.

"You take the pen," Cherokee said to me.

Nobody moved. Nobody spoke. I took the pen and bent across the gun, my ear lost in a wilderness of whiskers, my eyes looking out and up at the strange array of desperadoes with guns in their hands and strangely sorrowful looks in their eyes. Behind them were the powder kegs. The preacher still held the Bible. And I am sure they must have thought that old man Sheldon had died and I was going to stand there over that gun, the pen in my hand, looking at them for all eternity. And I would have settled for that myself. I would gladly have stood there the rest of my life if I could have avoided scratching out the words that came stinging like a bullet through the whiskers to my ear. For old man Sheldon finally rasped it out. "Marshal Geoffrey Tolliver," he said.

And so I stood, innocent scratcher of dread and doom, unable to scratch, looking, thinking, disbelieving, yet knowing it was the truth and therefore dying a little, doing just about everything but scratching out the name, which, once written, could never be recalled. All the pictures of him would have to come down. All the books would have to be redone. A lot of lives—my own especially—might have to be relived. I even wondered vaguely if maybe the shotgun would go off and the dynamite explode, taking all of us with it, so I would be spared the scratching of that name. And then rather crazily I thought, *Truth is not the most beautiful thing in the world*, while at the same time thinking that my hand might rebel and write some other name, some name unknown and uncared about by men. At the very least my hand might scrawl it so it would be unreadable. I was actually marveling at the shameful things that I could do, all of them seeming bright and pure and shining when compared with the truth I had to scratch. And all the time I was looking up at the guns, at the outlaws, at the marshals, at the horses, at Cherokee, and all of them were looking back, waiting for the scratch from

117

my reluctant hand. I even remembered certain words from his book, as, for example, "The truth will always come out, sooner or later, one way or another." True, I thought, and what a shame. Other words of his came into my mind. "Never tamper with a man's reputation. Keep out of Goodbye Gulch." Now that was good advice. I should have taken it. And that was when I got a glimmer, for the first time, of why he had said it. Up here, in Goodbye Gulch, *they knew. They had always known.* And I think it was there that things began to fall into place. It seemed strange that they could fall so fast and fit so neatly. I, still not scratching, just looking up at Dick Creel from my crazy, bent-over position, said, "Then he *was* Anonymous."

"That's right. Wrote the book himself."

"Who put in the deathbed words?"

"He wrote them too, long before he died."

"Was he . . ." I hesitated, not certain how to put it. "Was he as good when he was bad as he was when he was good?"

"Every bit of it."

I believed it. That was the part the outlaws wanted to remember. One good man. Outlaw or not, it didn't matter. *So long as there's just one man to put your faith in.*

Still bent over, still looking up, still not scratching, I said, "Then he was a U.S. marshal when he did it."

"Covered with glory," Dick Creel said.

Just one question remained. Just one word. Funny, I thought, how it always comes down to that one short word that the human mouth forms so softly. "Why?"

"Because the tax collector was a crook. If ever a man deserved it, he did."

"But crooks—especially crooks, laws are made for crooks—deserve a judge and a jury and a trial and a lawyer." I could feel my voice tightening, rising.

"He had all those things," Creel said. "The marshal was the judge and the jury and the lawyer for both sides."

"Took the law into his own hands," I said.

"Sometimes you have to," Dick Creel said.

Before I could change my mind, I scratched the name of Marshal Geoffrey Tolliver on the paper. It was, I knew, the truth. It was, I also knew, pure treason.

"There's something I ought to tell you," Dick Creel said.

"Yeah, what's that?" Nothing Dick Creel could say now would bother me.

"You're not gettin' out of the gulch alive with that confession."

I looked at him. I knew he meant it, but somehow it just didn't seem important. "You're forgettin' somethin', Marshal."

"What's that?"

"That horse there."

"And you're forgettin' somethin' else," old man Sheldon said. "I ain't dead yet, and this shotgun is still loaded. So, back off."

I motioned to Cherokee, and we walked around the shotgun to the horses. The guns all turned in unison as we went. When we were in the saddle, I said, "Marshal, this confession is going to Judge Docker. In the words of

Geoffrey Tolliver, duty is duty, no matter how much it hurts you."

I didn't know how much it hurt Dick Creel, but I knew how much it hurt me.

We turned then and rode out. About halfway up the canyon we heard them coming. I guessed old man Sheldon had given us what he figured was a fair start before layin' his head down on that shotgun for the final time.

15 ★ Bitin' the Bullet

It was a night to remember. Cherokee and I thundered toward Dead Horse Crossing, running for our lives. In my saddlebags the sacks of money chinked, and in hers the confession rested safely in the hymnbook. There was not a chance that the marshals could catch us before we reached the river, and once we were on the other side they would not pursue, it being a place too full of judges and juries and lawyers and hangmen's knots and other terrors of civilization.

Bullet Proof was tearing at the bit, as if saying please, let me show you how fast I can run. I held him in. Cherokee's horse was already doing its best, and I wanted us to hit that crossing side by side. We were going out the way we had come in, running. Tornadoes and renegade marshals. A part of the Territory. I knew as we ran that the marshals were deadly serious in their last desperate effort to recapture the vanishing remnant of their dreams—the model U.S. marshal, uncorrupted and incorruptible. *As long as there's just one man to put your faith in.* And I knew better than Dick Creel that he was right. But even knowing it, I wondered why always it was another man that men wanted to put their faith in. Why not put your faith in yourself? Why not you yourself be uncorrupted and incorruptible? Of course, it was fifty years too late for them to do that, and you began to feel a little sorry for them as you looked over your shoulder to see the pitiful race they were running in their attempt to recapture the dreams we had filched. Nothing, I felt, would make them happier than to die in the attempt to get the confession back, to ride their horses to death, if necessary. It was like dying for honor and pride, the last little speck of honor and pride, but still honor and pride.

Dead Horse Crossing was coming up fast. There were no signs of the campfires we had seen there earlier that evening. It looked like all we had to do was hit the water, reach a sand bar, and then run on to safety. Cherokee shouted something like, "We're going to make it!" Her voice was wild and joyous. I shouted back across the wind, "You're right!"

But she was wrong.

Oh, so wrong. Two horses loomed up out of the night, blocking Dead Horse Crossing. Then I remembered Fats and Grunt, missing from the cave. I should have thought of that, but I had had so little time to think. And now I had even less. In fact, I had none at all. We were bearing down upon them at a terrifying rate, Cherokee a little in back of me. And that was when I noticed that Bullet Proof actually had the bit betweeen his teeth now and was raging headlong at the two horses. I couldn't have held him if I had tried. A bullet went wild over our heads, but there was no time to think about that either. For right then Bullet Proof crashed straight into one horse and sideswiped the other, almost dragging my left leg off as he went. He stumbled a little, and maybe he even wobbled, but he never slowed, hitting the water with a violent splash. Cherokee's horse hit in a splash behind me, and somehow I knew two things. One, by the massive lump on that horse we had run over, I knew the rider could have been no other than Marshal Fats Tubstyle, while from the choked cry of the rider we had sideswiped, I knew he could only have been Hector Grunt. And the other thing I knew was my left leg was mangled. For some reason I couldn't think of anything except how hard it must be to get off and on a horse when you've got a mangled leg. The thought had never occurred to me before.

Into the river then, mangled leg and all, Cherokee now back beside me. We were out almost in the middle of the stream, the water only about four feet deep. That was when we heard the marshals shoutin' and firin' at us from the crossing.

"We're all right!" I shouted. "They won't try to cross the river. If we can make the other side, we're safe."

But now I was wrong. In every way.

Those old men, determined to the end, came plunging right on into the river, shoutin' and shootin'. That was one way I was wrong. And the other way was, the safety of the opposite bank. Oh, how wrong I was about that! There, out of the night, directly ahead of us, two or three figures loomed up. And then I remembered—the posse night guard, the drunken deputy who even when sober in daylight, which was rare, couldn't tell an innocent man from another.

That was when something hit me in the shoulder,

spinning me half out of the saddle, and I heard the sound of firing from ahead.

"Drunk men ahead and crazy men behind!" I shouted. "Head upstream!"

Bullet Proof bolted, straight up the river, Cherokee's horse stayin' close. Through my head, to the sound of more gunfire, went such words as "quagmire" and "quicksand" and other terrors of the Nescatunga River. It was about that time that something seemed to give way underfoot and we eased down deep into the water. It took me a moment to realize that Bullet Proof was swimming.

Cherokee did it right, sliding off her horse and hanging to the tail, but for me there could be no sliding. If I slid off, I'd never get back on.

Behind us the gunfire was still going on. The drunks and the crazies were shootin' it out . . . over, I thought, absolutely nothing. It looked like we had made it after all, if we didn't get drowned. Bullet Proof had his head up high, but most of his body was under. Those nine sacks of money, plus me, weren't helping him any. Cherokee's horse was pretty well under too. I couldn't see anything but his head and, back at the end of his tail, her. My head seemed to be doing funny things. My eyes seemed to be seein' and not seein'.

Then I noticed that Bullet Proof was walking again and Cherokee was back on her horse. I hadn't seen her get back on, so I guessed my head really was doing funny things and I wasn't seeing everything that happened. A little after that we were going up the bank and into a canyon leading upward to the top of a small mesa.

There, water still dripping from horses and riders, we stopped. The gulch was quiet now. Down below, the river ran silently.

"You all right?" I asked.

"Just wet. How about you?"

"Something's wrong with my leg."

"You're holding your arm."

"Something's wrong with it, too."

"Hang on," she said.

"I will."

And somehow I did. We moved on over the mesa until we reached the brush and pasture land, my head still doing funny things. It was a little before dawn when Cherokee said, "This will do," and got off her horse. Then she said, "Lean over on your good-leg side and fall on my shoulders."

Sweet consideration in her voice. Sweet consideration in mine too. "I weigh a hundred and twenty-seven pounds," I said.

She paid no attention, but half dragged and half carried me down from the saddle, all my limbs seeming to flop a little. My foot especially felt floppy and cold.

Leaning me against a rock, she said, "It's about half torn off."

"My leg?"

"Your boot." She took what was left of the boot and held it up. The sole was ripped half away and the upper looked like it had been run through a dull meat grinder. Also there was something white like a rock on what was left of the toe. Seemed imbedded there.

"What's that?"

She picked at it until it came, then held it up. "A tooth," she said.

"Horse or human?"

"Human."

And we both said it together, "Grunt!" I must have kicked him in the mouth when the horses collided.

Cherokee was feeling my foot and leg. "Wiggle your toes," she said.

I wiggled.

"They wiggle," she said. "Nothing's broken."

My leg began to unmangle pretty fast then. I guessed the flopping boot and bare toes had put a little scare in me. But that bullet wound in my shoulder was the real thing. I could feel the blood dripping down my sleeve. That drunken deputy had managed to do what all the marshals and outlaws of Goodbye Gulch couldn't do—shoot me.

"I'll swab it down," Cherokee said, ripping off about half my shirt. "Pity we didn't keep a little of that whisky. Sterilizes good. The shroud would come in handy too."

"Is it that bad?" I asked, glad she hadn't mentioned the spade.

"I meant for bandages."

"I thought women used their petticoats."

"You're gettin' delirious," she said, ripping the shirt in strips and beginning to swab the wound.

I guessed I was. I knew she was wearing Mr. Levi's specials, the kind with rivets in them. But a little faintness had relaxed me, and I felt the need to use warm and proper phrases for the work at hand. It was, after all, my first bullet wound. Blood, pure blood—my blood—

was dripping down my arm and curling around my ribs. I had been shot by a drunken deputy, and a beautiful Indian girl was leaning over me with wet cloths of mercy in her hands. To the west the rimrocks. To the south the Rio Grande.

"Lay your cool hand on my brow," I said.

"Delirious," she said, but on my brow she put a cool wet cloth, which, though not her hand, felt good.

"That eases me," I said, "as does the music that I hear. That comes from Mexico. They call it 'La Golondrina.'"

To the west the rimrocks. To the south the Rio Grande.

"Delirious."

But she didn't ruin my moment. She let me have my rimrocks and my music. She let my beautiful horse lower his nose at me and snort, soft messy objects of his love a-spray upon my face. She even let me lament the missing spade and shroud, which I adorned with loving care in muttered offerings. It would have been better—for my appearance—if she hadn't used up most of my shirt for swabs, and I could have wished while lying there looking at my toes that I had two boots on instead of one, if things went wrong. Those bare toes seemed so fragile and undefended in the morning sunrise—at the mercy of the world. But all in all I was happy in my haziness, except for an occasional moment when things seemed to be going not according to the rules . . . as for instance when she put the leather rein in my mouth and said, "Clamp your teeth on it if the pain gets too bad."

How was she to know I was supposed to bite a bullet

in that moment? And where, except for the one in my shoulder, would she have found one? So I clamped my teeth upon the rein and looked at my naked toes, wishing I had worn socks, and felt the tip of the blade of my own knife, in her hand against my flesh, and heard her say, after the world had spun a little, "I got it," and saw her holding up the bullet for my admiration—a bloody chunk of lead it was—so I said through the rein in my mouth, "Thanks, Cherokee."

"Don't mention it, Territory." Then she started ripping at the other half of my shirt to use for binding me up, saying, "If I only had some willow bark and powdered dung like the old folks use . . ."

"Do the Osages use it?"

"They discovered it."

"Then look in my shirt pocket, if the pocket's still there."

It was still there. She took out the packet and held it up. "Your Osage friend," she said. And then, "How did he know?"

"I'll never know," I said, knowing it was the truth.

She went to work applying the herbs and dung.

A little later, when I was sitting up and not so hazy in the head, she fashioned a sling from our bandannas. Then she said, "Wiggle your fingers."

I wiggled.

"They wiggle," she said. "No broken bones. How do you feel?"

"I miss my boot."

"Do you still hear music?"

"It's gettin' fainter. How we fixed for water?"

"Don't think we got any."

She went over to her horse and took down the saddle-bags and started to take out the canteen. Then she stopped, suddenly. Then she looked at me. Then she lifted up the saddlebags and poured the contents on the ground, beside my bootless foot. The contents turned out to be mostly water . . . river water, salt water, from the Nescatunga. But that wasn't what caused us—humans and horses alike—to stare at each other across what you might call the space of disbelief. What caused that was the hymnbook. It came floating out with the rest of the objects. From inside the cover of the book came the confession . . . or what was left of it. Not only was the ink gone, blended into unreadable blots, the paper itself was falling to watery pieces in her hands. That was one confession no one would ever read.

16 ★ Right and Proper

To the west the rimrocks. The sun was hot and high. Cherokee and I walked our horses over the buffalo grass toward the junction of two old Osage trails where we would say goodbye, she to head west for Rimrock City, I south to Bitter Wells. The sacks of money chinked in my saddlebags. Any stranger seeing us would have needed only a glance to decide that we were running from the law and that we were paying a pretty high price for doing it. "Gone bad," he might have said as he rode away. "A couple of young'ns." You couldn't have blamed him.

At the junction of the trails, we stopped. The horses stood quietly, stomping a little against the flies and snortin' at nothin' in particular.

"Want me to ride a ways with you?" I asked.

"No. You're hurtin'. I can tell."

"Not much."

"Suppose he wants to run?" she asked, meaning Bullet Proof.

"He knows I'm hurt."

"There's something I've got to say," she said.

I waited.

"We lost," she said.

"Everybody lost."

"There's something I've got to ask," she said.

I waited.

"Was he a kin of yours, the man whose name you wrote?"

"Not by blood."

"I'll ride a little ways with you," she said.

"No. I've got to do the rest of it alone."

"I understand." She paused, then said, "There's something I've got to do."

I waited.

She leaned across, close. And I was looking into the eyes of Cherokee Waters. *Cherokee Waters ... Cherokee Waters ... youngest and fairest of Moonon's daughters ... With a name like that you didn't even need a guitar. You could just cry it to the rimrocks and the buffalo grass.* For once there wasn't a shotgun or a sack of money or a dying man or a grunting desperado between us. There was nothing between us but my wounded arm and the colliding brims of our hats, which did nothing to keep us apart. What wounded arm would dare feel pain in such a moment? "Goodbye, Territory Gore," she said. And she headed west for the rimrocks, fast, not looking back.

"Goodbye, Cherokee Waters," I said softly to the wind.

It was, then, as it had been at the first, Bullet Proof and I alone. I had only one thing left to do—the last act, so to speak, not of my life but of my beleaguered youth. I wanted to do it right and proper. I *had* to do it right and proper. Then and only then would it all be over with.

Gritting my teeth a little against the returning pain, I rode slowly on across the buffalo grass to do what I had to do.

Late that afternoon Bullet Proof—glint-eyed again now, head held high—walked down the dusty street in Bitter Wells. I sat tall, as tall as I could manage, in the saddle, shirtless, one arm in a sling, one boot flopping. I looked neither to the right nor to the left. Quite a few people were congregated in the street, some in front of the bank demanding their money and some in front of the Paradise Saloon demanding credit. The two crowds were about equal in size and—as I had known since my childhood—devotion. Bullet Proof swung his head majestically and came to a stop in front of the hitching post, snortin' noisily. There, in their customary circle, stood the mayor, the sheriff, the drunken deputy, the doctor, the barber, the preacher, and the undertaker. Their faces were long, their spirits low. They saw me, and yet it seemed they didn't see me, as if their eyes were seeing other things and their minds were elsewhere. Finally, a little absent-mindedly, the mayor looked at me and said hello. Then he said, "The bank was robbed, Territory. We're ruined."

I didn't answer.

"We chased 'em all over the gulch," the sheriff said.

I didn't answer.

"I winged one of them," the drunken deputy said, "but he got away. Wherever he is, he's got a bullet in him."

I didn't answer. Then I twisted a little to get the saddlebags from behind me. The nine sacks made a heavy load as I swung them around, but I would have died before showing any pain. Then, in one final heave, I tossed the moneybags at their feet.

The marshal sat in the saddle, wounded, tired, dirty, tobacco juice staining the edges of his drooping mustache. He sat quietly, listening to the people marvel at what he had done single-handed at the risk of his life. He didn't pay much attention to them. Just dropped the sacks of money to the ground, wiped a little dried blood from off his arm, and looked off toward the rim-rocks.

When the money hit the ground, there was a little chorus of oohs and ahs. I was ready for that too. I sat the saddle and listened to the voices warm with praise and admiration. There were blessings from the preacher, blessings from the banker, from the sheriff and under-taker. There were blessings from those devoted to money and those devoted to the whisky it would buy. They swarmed around, but not too close, Bullet Proof's glinting eye becoming ever so slightly murderous.

And finally it came . . . the moment, the only time it would ever come to me. When the mayor began to marvel at the beauty of my deed, mentioning as he did so the bitter wounds I obviously had suffered, and his praises reached the point where my horse and I were both embarrassed, I looked past him toward the rimrocks and the mesas, then looked back down, and said, "It goes with the Territory."

And oh how I wished I had a long drooping mustache with tobacco stains around the edge.

⋆ About the Author

Rex Benedict writes that his biography can best be set forth in periods:

"There was the Oklahoma Period, where I was born and raised; the Northwestern State College Period, where I was educated; the U.S. Navy Period, where I flew from aircraft carriers; the European Period, where I translated and dubbed movies; the Greek and Roman Revival Period, where I pined among the relics; the Freighter Period, where I cruised endlessly on blue seas; the Corsair Press Period, where I privately published my greatest works and gave them all away; the Translation Period, where I translated many books, including *The Decameron*, into many languages, hopefully the right ones; the Juvenile Novel Period, where I astounded myself and others by writing Westerns; and finally the Terrace Period, where I now sit on West 88th Street in New York City, marveling at it all."

TITLES IN THE NEW WINDMILL SERIES

Chinua Achebe: *Things Fall Apart*
Louisa M. Alcott: *Little Women*
Elizabeth Allen: *Deitz and Denny*
Margery Allingham: *The Tiger in the Smoke*
Michael Anthony: *The Year in San Fernando*
Enid Bagnold: *National Velvet*
Stan Barstow: *Joby*
H. Mortimer Batten: *The Singing Forest*
Nina Bawden: *On the Run; The Witch's Daughter; A Handful of Thieves;
    Carrie's War*
Phyllis Bentley: *The Adventures of Tom Leigh*
Paul Berna: *Flood Warning*
Pierre Boulle: *The Bridge on the River Kwai*
E. R. Braithwaite: *To Sir, With Love*
D. K. Broster: *The Flight of the Heron; The Gleam in the North; The Dark Mile*
F. Hodgson Burnett: *The Secret Garden*
Helen Bush: *Mary Anning's Treasures*
A. Calder-Marshall: *The Man from Devil's Island*
John Caldwell: *Desperate Voyage*
Albert Camus: *The Outsider*
Victor Canning: *The Runaways; Flight of the Grey Goose*
Erskine Childers: *The Riddle of the Sands*
John Christopher: *The Guardians; The Lotus Caves*
Richard Church: *The Cave; Over the Bridge; The White Doe*
Colette: *My Mother's House*
Lettice Cooper: *The Twig of Cypress*
Alexander Cordell: *The Traitor Within*
Meindert deJong: *The Wheel on the School*
Peter Dickinson: *The Gift*
Eleanor Doorly: *The Radium Woman; The Microbe Man; The Insect Man*
Gerald Durrell: *Three Singles to Adventure; The Drunken Forest; Encounters
    with Animals*
Elizabeth Enright: *Thimble Summer; The Saturdays*
C. S. Forester: *The General*
Eve Garnett: *The Family from One End Street; Further Adventures of the Family
    from One End Street; Holiday at the Dew Drop Inn*
G. M. Glaskin: *A Waltz through the Hills*
Rumer Godden: *Black Narcissus*
Margery Godfrey: *South for Gold*
Angus Graham: *The Golden Grindstone*
Graham Greene: *The Third Man* and *The Fallen Idol*
Grey Owl: *Sajo and her Beaver People*
G. and W. Grossmith: *The Diary of a Nobody*
René Guillot: *Kpo the Leopard*
Esther Hautzig: *The Endless Steppe*
Jan De Hartog: *The Lost Sea*
Erik Haugaard: *The Little Fishes*
Bessie Head: *When Rain Clouds Gather*
John Hersey: *A Single Pebble*

Georgette Heyer: *Regency Buck*

Alfred Hitchcock: *Sinister Spies*

C. Walter Hodges: *The Overland Launch*

Geoffrey Household: *Rogue Male; A Rough Shoot; Prisoner of the Indies*

Fred Hoyle: *The Black Cloud*

Irene Hunt: *Across Five Aprils*

Henry James: *Washington Square*

Josephine Kamm: *Young Mother; Out of Step; Where Do We Go From Here?; The Starting Point*

Erich Kästner: *Emil and the Detectives*

John Knowles: *A Separate Peace*

D. H. Lawrence: *Sea and Sardinia; The Fox* and *The Virgin and the Gipsy; Selected Tales*

Marghanita Laski: *Little Boy Lost*

Harper Lee: *To Kill a Mockingbird*

Laurie Lee: *As I Walked Out One Mid-Summer Morning*

Ursula Le Guin: *A Wizard of Earthsea; The Tombs of Atuan; The Farthest Shore*

Doris Lessing: *The Grass is Singing*

C. Day Lewis: *The Otterbury Incident*

Lorna Lewis: *Leonardo the Inventor*

Martin Lindsay: *The Epic of Captain Scott*

David Line: *Run for Your Life*

Kathleen Lines: *The House of the Nightmare; The Haunted and the Haunters*

Joan Lingard: *Across the Barricades*

Penelope Lively: *The Ghost of Thomas Kempe*

Jack London: *The Call of the Wild; White Fang*

Carson McCullers: *The Member of the Wedding*

Lee McGiffen: *On the Trail to Sacramento*

Wolf Mankowitz: *A Kid for Two Farthings*

Olivia Manning: *The Play Room*

James Vance Marshall: *A River Ran Out of Eden*

David Martin: *The Cabby's Daughter*

J. P. Martin: *Uncle*

John Masefield: *Sard Harker; The Bird of Dawning; The Midnight Folk; The Box of Delights*

W. Somerset Maugham: *The Kite and Other Stories*

Guy de Maupassant: *Prisoners of War and Other Stories*

Laurence Meynell: *Builder and Dreamer*

Yvonne Mitchell: *Cathy Away*

Honoré Morrow: *The Splendid Journey*

Bill Naughton: *The Goalkeeper's Revenge*

E. Nesbit: *The Railway Children; The Story of the Treasure Seekers*

E. Neville: *It's Like this, Cat*

Wilfrid Noyce: *South Col*

Robert C. O'Brien: *Mrs Frisby and the Rats of NIMH; Z for Zachariah*

Scott O'Dell: *Island of the Blue Dolphins*

George Orwell: *Animal Farm*

Merja Otava: *Priska*

John Prebble: *The Buffalo Soldiers*

J. B. Priestley: *Saturn Over the Water*